A NOVEL

Bloodlust

K.B.
CASIMIR

First published in the United States 2024
This paperback edition published 2024

ISBN: PB: 979-8-218-39452-3; e-Book: 979-8-218-39453-0

Cover and formatting by Books and Moods

To my best friend Becca, who was taken too soon from this world. Without you, I would not be the writer I am today and this novel would not be possible. I hope you're sleeping well. I miss you sorely.

"For the *last* time, I'm not coming to your party. I don't care who's going to be there."

Sebastian stared at his friend and widened his eyes. Charlotte had just invited him to yet another one of her balls she felt compelled to throw. He turned her down almost always, but they had a running deal that he had to agree at least once a year to be social with her. The year was drawing to a close and he knew she'd throw that wager right back in his face should he decline again.

Which, she did.

"*Please*, Sebby? Remember our deal? Once a—"

"Yes, yes," Sebastian groaned. "Fine. If I come to this, no more badgering until next October. All of New Orleans is going to be there, I assume?"

"Not this time. Inner circle only, darling," Charlotte said with a grin, before patting his cheek. "Tonight at seven. But for you, six. I need to make sure you look presentable, and you're going to need someone to do your hair. You can borrow some of Vic's clothes."

Sebastian moved his face away from her hand and cut his eyes to another part of the room. He narrowly resisted grumbling under his breath.

Sebastian sat at home, contemplating the ramifications of not going to this party. Charlotte Labasque was a force to be reckoned with when scorned, and if he pissed her off enough, she'd sic her husband Victor after him. She knew it would work, too, because Sebastian was a slave to their friendship.

He'd met Victor Labasque when he was 11 years old. Food wasn't easy to come by in his household, so when he was old enough, he resorted to a life of petty crime to get some cash. His father didn't have much time for anything other than drinking, sometimes making it to work, and taking out his frustrations on his wife and only child. His mother wasn't much better. Though she was not an alcoholic, she self-medicated in other ways, and Sebastian was sure she got attention from other men to pass the time. They were so absorbed in their own crises that they often forgot Sebastian existed.

He preferred it that way after a while. It made things easier.

It had been all he'd ever known growing up, so he didn't often voice it or complain about it. At first, he thought it was normal, given he'd never done anything wrong to warrant that kind of behavior. Not that that sort of behavior was excusable for any reason, no matter how bad, but still. He'd been a child and had spent years wondering why he wasn't good enough for them. As he'd grown older, and gone to school, he realized his life was not normal at all, and had let his situation slip to his first-grade teacher. She rightfully reported it to the principal, who in turn reported it to the authorities to investigate. When the police and child services showed up at the house, and his parents found out what he'd done, all hell broke loose. Sebastian still wasn't too sure how his mother convinced the government investigators to let him stay at the house, but Sebastian always assumed she just gave a sob story. You'd think they'd be immune to that sort of thing, but... things were different in Louisiana. After that, his father had beaten him within an inch of his life and told him, "The next time you do that, you won't be waking up."

He hadn't said a word ever again. Not for another near-decade — until he met Victor.

He and the blonde boy had clicked instantaneously and had been attached at the hip for the rest of their lives. Sebastian was sure he would have been locked away or worse had it not been for the Labasques' intervention. Charlotte coming into their lives years later only made things better. Sebastian would be lost without them. They had dragged him out of his life of crime and convinced him he could be more than just a carbon copy of his father.

They also opened his eyes to the fact that New Orleans could be more than a dirty city filled with crime. Victor especially exposed him to the rich culture steeped within every corner of their beautiful hometown. There had been a time when Sebastian couldn't wait to get the hell out of the South, and now he couldn't imagine being anywhere else. It was still dirty and there was plenty of crime, but the pretty and ugly of the Big Easy were what made it one-of-a-kind.

Though Sebastian often put up a front of being inconvenienced by all of Charlotte or Victor's shenanigans, he would do anything in the world they asked. He owed them that much, but one thing he always appreciated about them was that they never made him *feel* like he owed them. They would do the most generous things for him, like give him a place to stay, stock his fridge with food when his work was slow, or even force him to go get a haircut because he was always going to 'do it next week.' They would take care of him like he was their own blood, and never ask for a thing in return. It was almost as natural as breathing for them. The least Sebastian could do was go to a few of their parties when they begged him to.

And he never said no to good food and free booze.

Sebastian walked down the sidewalk, the cool breeze biting around him. He didn't live far from the Labasques, but he certainly didn't live in the same fashion. He lived in a one-bedroom shotgun duplex next to an elderly woman who, he was almost positive, was scared of him. Sebastian wasn't sure he had the whole 'starving artist' persona down just yet, but as a freelance photographer in an over-saturated market trying to make ends meet, he felt like he was getting there.

Rounding the corner, he approached Labasque Manor, as they so humbly called it. It was a two-story home, all white on the outside, with black accents. A black, iron-wrought fence surrounded it with gold fleur de lis topping each spike. The garden in front was always immaculately kept, even in the short cold months the South was graced with. Short hedges lined parts of the yard around the sides of the house, leading anyone who was welcomed into a large courtyard and garden in the back.

He let himself in, the gate creaking as he closed it. He hadn't bothered to wear anything nice of his own or do anything except wash his hair, because he knew Charlotte would take over and order him to change.

Sebastian unlocked the door and walked in, closing it behind himself. "Charlie?" he called out.

A blonde head popped out over the stair railing from above. "Good, you're here. Come on, we don't have time to waste."

Sebastian obeyed and walked up the steps to her room. She and Victor had their own bedroom, of course, but Charlotte also had a room solely for her clothes and makeup.

Admittedly, Victor had one too.

"What are you feeling tonight, Sebby? The usual gothic intimidation, I'm guessing? You know, that's *absolutely* why you don't have a girlfriend," Charlotte said as she sifted through a few things she'd grabbed from Victor's closet.

"I'm not sure those two things correlate, but yes, I suppose the 'usual gothic intimidation' will be fine," Sebastian said, sinking into the bed while watching her. "Can we not just do a normal black suit? Nothing wrong with a classic."

"It's *boring*, Sebastian. You are not boring. *We* are not boring," Charlotte huffed, before pulling out a suit that Sebastian was sure cost more than he made in a year. "Put this one on. It's black, like you like, but the stitching is silver. It'll give you a little *oomph*."

"I prefer to be oomphless," Sebastian drawled. His eyes scanned over the suit as he took it from her. It was nice, but he didn't expect anything less. Everything they owned was nice.

Charlotte ignored his snark and settled for rolling her eyes. "Do you want your hair up or down?"

"Is the great Charlotte Labasque giving me a *choice*? I may throw a parade downstairs," Sebastian said, biting back a smirk at her unamused expression. "Down is fine."

"Another reason you don't have a girlfriend," she muttered, gesturing for him to undress and change. "You're an asshole."

"*Thank you*," Sebastian said with a smile and a small dip of his head. "That means so much coming from you."

"*Strip!*"

Sebastian did as told and pulled on the suit. It felt nice, as they always did, and for once, he liked what he saw in the mirror. He ran his hands down over the front, noting how soft the material was. The details were fine, and he couldn't help but wonder what sort of special guests they expected tonight, and why the hell they'd want him to be a part of it. This was nice even for their standards.

Charlotte moved him into a chair in front of her vanity and immediately began running a brush through his dark hair. It snagged slightly on the waves, but humidity did that no matter how many times he brushed it. He stared at her in the mirror as her hands made quick work of products he'd already lost count of.

"Do I get to know anything about tonight?" Sebastian finally asked.

Charlotte sighed and focused on his hair. "It will be me, you, Victor, and three very important guests. Plus... a few others who will simply serve to fill the room."

"Who are these three very important people?"

Charlotte hesitated, which he found odd. Eventually, she spoke. "They have a lifestyle that Victor and I would like to be a part of."

"Why are you being so cryptic?" Sebastian asked, then winced as she tugged on his hair, curling it around her iron.

"Because I don't think you'll approve, but I'm hoping they can convince you."

Sebastian stayed quiet for a moment, trying to figure out her labyrinth of an explanation — if you could even call it an explanation. It was more like a riddle. "Why wouldn't I approve? I don't even live the same lifestyle you and Victor have. What makes you think I would be deigned important enough to live a lifestyle that *you* covet?"

"You are special, Sebby. I wish you'd stop saying that about yourself," she sighed. "I just wanted you to meet them and hear them out. Okay? Really hear them out. I know you don't really believe in some things, but—"

"Oh, God," Sebastian groaned. "Are they some sort of religious cult?"

"Not exactly," Charlotte said shortly. "You'll see."

Sebastian knew the conversation was over. Usually, Charlotte was the one who told him everything in excruciating detail, even if he didn't ask. He knew far too much about his best friends' life in the bedroom than he'd *ever* wanted. He had noticed her body language change and stiffen when he'd asked, so he assumed she was serious about this meeting.

2

他room hummed with music and chatter as the
party continued in full swing.

Outside, three women walked through the gate,
but a redheaded one stopped the other two.

"Why are we doing this again?" she asked.

"Leona, they *want* to be like us. I have spent a lot of time
around them, I think they could be good additions to the
coven. They're wealthy, they understand the need for secrecy,
and they seem to be like-minded to us. I wanted you to meet
them. Whitney approves," the blonde woman said.

Between them, a brunette woman spoke next, nodding
her head in agreement. "They're the ones we've been telling
you about. I think you'll like them."

Leona shook her head and folded her arms. "You know I
don't like shit like this."

"You used to love parties and dances and being social,"
the blonde said. "Try to have fun. You can't let a dark cloud

loom over you forever. Just remember: 'WWPD.'"

"What the hell is 'WWPD?'" Leona asked.

"'What Would Piper Do?'" she said with a laugh.

"Okay, just because I need to see people other than you due to *that*, I'll go in," Leona teased.

Piper gave a small noise of excitement and looped arms with the other women.

They entered.

Leona looked around the ornate entryway that led to what must be a ballroom. It reminded her of her childhood. The balls her parents would throw and she'd sneak out and watch from the upper floor. She'd always dreamed of the day she was old enough to be a part of them, and when she turned sixteen, she was.

It had been the worst mistake of her existence.

"There they are," Piper said, pulling her friends with her.

"Hello, darling," Charlotte said as she leaned forward to embrace Piper, the blondes both exchanging kisses to the cheek. "Glad you came."

"Of course," Piper said. "You know Whitney, of course, but this is—"

"Leona Abrin," Victor then chimed in smoothly, giving her a rehearsed smile. "We have heard so much about you. I'm Victor Labasque, this is my wife Charlotte."

"Pleasure," Leona said, not taking the outstretched hands in front of her. "I need a drink and someone to dance on," she mumbled, moving past them and through the crowd.

Whitney shot the Labasques an apologetic look. "You'll have to excuse her. It's been a while since she's been to a party.

She's…"

"Prickly," Piper finished, smirking to herself. "She'll loosen up. Anyway," she sighed, looking around. "This is quite the party. You didn't go to all this trouble for us, did you?"

"Of course we did," Charlotte said. "We want to show you that we're serious. And we want Leona to like us. And…" she said as she turned a bit, her eyes darting around the room. She then looked up at her husband. "Where's Sebastian?"

"Lurking somewhere probably," Victor muttered.

"Who's Sebastian?" Whitney asked.

"Our closest friend. We wanted you to meet him tonight. Vic, can you go find him?" she asked. "We aren't sure if he'd also be interested, but… we feel responsible for him. Either way, he ought to be in the loop."

"We didn't discuss another person," Piper said. "We don't even know this man."

"You will," Victor said, then he disappeared to find his friend.

Sebastian peered down into his drink, wishing he was anywhere else but there. As usual, Charlotte and Victor had completely abandoned him to do God knows what. He could feel a headache coming on, which was stopping him from imbibing any more alcohol.

Though, these parties made for good people-watching. It was always the same caliber of people trying to get in good with his friends. He wondered if they had any shred of self-respect with the way they behaved.

"Where'd you get that drink?"

Sebastian jolted slightly and turned to face the most beautiful person he'd ever laid eyes on. He re-focused and processed her question. "Kitchen," he simply said.

Leona tilted her head slightly, staring at him intently. There was something about this man that seemed familiar to her, but she couldn't put her finger on it. He was a human, that much she could tell. The only immortals in the building were her coven. "Are you going to show me where the kitchen is?"

Sebastian furrowed his brows and lifted the hand holding his drink to the room adjacent to the one they were in. "If you bothered to look around, it's right there."

Leona narrowly avoided smirking. "Aren't you the gentleman?"

Sebastian wasn't sure how to respond. Universes in which women this beautiful spoke to him merely didn't exist.

"There are also servers with drinks and hors d'oeuvres floating around. And bartenders."

"So why do you get the privilege of making your own drink?" Leona asked.

"Because nobody else makes it right and I don't enjoy speaking to most humans."

Leona *did* smile at that. "Is that so? Do you spend a lot of time speaking to non-humans then?"

Sebastian regarded her carefully. She was weird. But he'd play along. She hadn't walked away yet. "Oh, yes. New Orleans is full of my supernatural best friends. I have a date with a poltergeist in about an hour."

Leona laughed under her breath. "I won't keep you then. I'm—"

"Sebastian! There you are. I've been looking everywhere for you," Victor interrupted. "I see you've met Leona."

The dark-haired man looked down at the redhead. Leona. Interesting name. "I suppose I have," he said.

"Leona, this is Sebastian Beliveau. Mine and Charlotte's best friend. Sebastian, this is Leona Abrin. One of the guests we were telling you about," he said, giving him a pointed look.

"Ah," Sebastian merely said. "I was just telling her about your bartenders' lousy drinks."

Victor glared at him and pressed his lips together in a thin line. "Come, I want you to meet the others. Charlotte has requested your presence. Leona, will you be joining us?"

Leona sighed and lolled her head to one side. "I still don't have a drink."

"What would you like?" Victor asked, and then he hesitated. "Or…"

"Don't," Leona said, putting a hand up. "I'll make Sebastian fix me one in a minute," she said, eyeing him.

Sebastian tensed. Something about this woman unnerved him. He wanted to be as far away from her as possible.

He followed Victor and Leona to Charlotte and the others. They gave him the same sort of unwell feeling deep in the pit of his stomach. He liked to think he was a good judge of character, and it threw him off that three seemingly normal women could set him on edge so much.

"Finally," Charlotte said with a smile. She pulled

Sebastian closer by his arm and squeezed him next to her. "Sebastian, this is Piper Aldene and Whitney Blackwoode. I see you've already met Leona. Piper, Whitney, this is Sebastian Beliveau. The friend I was telling you about."

"You don't have to be scared of us," Piper said to him, gently shaking his hand. "We won't bite."

"Unless you ask," Leona said.

Sebastian looked between them, wondering what sort of alternate planet he'd fallen on. Why the hell did they want to be around these people? Why did they need any more *friends*?

"Let's go somewhere more private to talk," Victor suggested. "We can go to my study."

Knowing better than to try to escape, Sebastian followed. He walked in with them, Victor shutting the door behind them. He wanted to ask what was going on and why they were all acting so strangely, but he had better manners than that.

"Judging by the confused and downright unnerved look on Sebastian's face, I'm going to hedge a bet that you haven't told him any details?" Piper asked.

"We thought it would be better to let you explain. He wouldn't believe us," Charlotte answered.

Sebastian looked between them. He felt like the butt of a prank. "Believe what?"

"That we're vampires," Leona said. "And your friends want to become immortal. That's why they invited us."

ebastian stared at them, waiting for a punchline. A breathy, awkward laugh escaped his mouth, but when nobody else showed any sort of humor, his throat bobbed. "Have I been drugged?" he asked, looking down at his drink.

"Told you," Charlotte said, leaning against the edge of a desk. "Sebastian isn't spiritual. He doesn't believe in anything supernatural."

"You are crazy," Sebastian said, shaking his head. Many people in the city claimed to be vampires, but they were all on something. Many parts of the city gave into its haunted history, but it was just a bunch of scary stories.

"Are we?" Leona asked. "Shall we prove it to you?"

Instinctively, Sebastian backed up. He felt even worse now than he had when he'd met them. "I want to leave."

"We won't hurt you, Sebastian," Whitney said. "Promise."

"I didn't think you would," he responded. "But whatever

weird shit you've got going on, you aren't dragging *my* friends into it. They have too much to lose. Have you two lost your minds?" he asked, turning to the blondes.

"No, Bas," Victor said seriously. "We want this."

"Want *what*?!" Sebastian exclaimed, completely exasperated by this charade.

Leona rolled her eyes, tired of his skepticism. She moved faster than any human could and pushed Sebastian against the wall, a few things clattering around them from the force. Sebastian stared at her, eyes wide, and his drink tumbled from his hand. She smiled, and when she opened her mouth to speak, Sebastian noticed fangs that absolutely were *not* there before.

"Believe us now?" she whispered.

His heart raced, and he felt more terror than he'd ever experienced in his life. Could she hear his blood pumping? Could she sense how afraid he was—

"Yes, I can," Leona answered, which only made things worse.

"Let me go," Sebastian said, his voice wavering. "Let me go *now*."

Leona acquiesced and backed off. Sebastian rubbed his chest and tried to keep his breathing under control. Ten minutes ago, it had been a perfectly normal evening, albeit slightly torturous. Now, he was locked in a study with his two best friends and three vampires. Maybe he *had* been dropped off on an alternate planet. "Am I allowed to leave?" Sebastian asked quietly, his fists clenched together.

"Sebastian—"

"*Am I* — allowed to leave?" he repeated firmly. "Or are you going to kill me?"

"We're not killing anyone," Piper said. "And we aren't holding you hostage."

Sebastian didn't need to be told twice. He walked to the door and flung it open, before he left the party.

On the way home, he contemplated stopping in a bar and drinking himself silly; he decided against that.

For the first time in a long time, he felt like he was looking at his hometown in a completely new light. All of the spooky stories and crocks of shit people used to sucker drunk tourists into buying things all turned out to be... well, real. How was that *possible*? Why hadn't anyone found out about this? It was the 21st century, surely other people had come across these monsters? Creatures? Fiends? He wasn't sure the politically correct term for them.

He needed to know how the fuck his best friends had gotten roped into all this. He *certainly* needed to know how the fuck they had managed to get duped into wanting to be like them. Though that redheaded woman had literally slammed him up against the wall — something someone of her stature absolutely should not be able to do — he still was having a hard time believing everything. Were they really just on drugs? Maybe that woman was a bodybuilder and just hid it well? Maybe *he* had been drugged and all of this was some rancid fever dream?

Upon returning to his house, he paced back and forth, ignoring his phone buzzing in his pocket. He was sure one of them would follow him to his house at some point and try to make him see sense. He didn't know if any of this was sensical though. Putting aside the fact that vampires apparently existed, why would his friends want to die? Those women had seemed normal enough, but... they were monsters. Unnatural. *Murderers.* Victor and Charlotte weren't like that. He knew them, they wouldn't want this.

He had more questions than answers. In fact, he had *no* answers. What would happen if they actually went through with this? They would become immortal, blood-sucking demons, and he'd be left behind or killed. Didn't he mean anything to them? Didn't their families mean anything to them? Their *lives*?

Sebastian ran a shaky hand through his hair, then reached into his pocket. He pulled out a packet of cigarettes and plucked one at random. Stepping outside to his porch, he lit one up and took a long drag.

Everything he'd ever known in life was not true, apparently. He had never given into religion or superstitions, despite growing up in one of the most famously haunted cities in the world. He had never trusted in a higher power to grant his wishes or make his problems go away. He had never gone to get tarot cards read or invested in voodoo. Everything he had was off his own back. He worked hard for the life he led, and other than the sanctuary Victor offered him in his youth, he had been on his own all his life. He had found religious nuts idiotic and had laughed at the thought of attending church every Sunday to pray to a deity that turned the other cheek at dying children and starving nations. Perhaps it was all real. Hell was obviously real and walking among them. Perhaps God was just as evil as Satan.

He supposed God just must be a better con artist.

4

Sebastian woke up to a banging noise coming from the front of his house the next day. He looked over and checked his phone for the time. At the 5 in the hour's spot, he groaned. Who the hell was at his door before dawn?

Padding across the living room, he glanced out the small window pane beside the door. He frowned and felt his chest constrict before he slowly opened the door half a foot. "What do you want? Why are you here?"

"Not usually the response I get when I drop in on men," Leona said with a smirk. "You know I could just barge my way in, right?"

"So why don't you?"

"I like to think of myself as a lady."

Sebastian inched the door open wider but didn't make any sort of move to let her through. "You're a vampire. You have to be invited in, right? That's one of the myths."

"Aren't you full of fun facts? I like a well-read man," she teased. "Are you going to invite me in?"

"That depends," Sebastian drawled. "Are you going to eat me?"

"I'm watching my figure," Leona said. She waited for him to crack a smile, and when he didn't, she merely rolled her eyes and pushed past him. "You were right. The invitation-only thing is a *myth*. We can go where we please. It would be extremely cumbersome and annoying to have to wait to come in everywhere."

Sebastian knew it was pointless to try to kick her out. It was probably best he stayed on her good side. "You never answered my question earlier. Why are you here?"

"I thought it was rather rude that you stormed out last night. So judgmental. I'm sure your friends will come 'round later today when the sun's up. Daylight and I aren't on speaking terms at the moment," she said, perching on the arm of his sofa.

"So that's true, then? No sunlight? Do you crumble into ash?"

Leona laughed and shook her head. "Nothing so dramatic. If we're in direct sunlight, we burn pretty extensively. Imagine a sunburn times a hundred. We heal if we can get into the shade quick enough, but it doesn't feel nice."

"What if you wear sunscreen?"

"Mmm," Leona hummed, folding a leg over the other. "Doesn't really work. I've gotten used to the shadows anyway. Sleeves and a good hat work wonders. And gloomy days. We have a lot of those in England."

"That's where you're from?"

"The accent didn't give it away?"

Sebastian flushed and cut his eyes away. "Where in England?"

"London."

"Why are you *here*?"

"How many times are you going to ask that?" Leona asked, eyeing him closely. "If you mean New Orleans, I'm… taking care of personal matters. London is crowded," she said softly. "But as far as why I'm *here*, at your house, I wanted to talk to you. Obviously you're brimming with questions. I can practically hear your thoughts."

Sebastian brought a protective hand to his head. "You can read minds, too? Is there anything you can't do?"

"I can't *read* minds. I can't hear every line that goes through your head. It's tough to explain. *But*, I can't get drunk," Leona said. "I can drink and eat human food, but it does nothing for me. It's strange," she sighed, sliding to sit down properly on the sofa. "Without a functioning liver — or any other organs — it doesn't have the same effect on me. It makes it easy to blend in though. This place has immaculate food. Very French."

"Some of it," he muttered. "What about garlic?"

Leona made a face. "Not my thing. Doesn't kill me, just… I hate it. Always have."

He was making mental notes. "Silver?"

"I prefer gold."

"Stake to the heart?"

"Stake to the heart kills anything, not just us."

Sebastian couldn't counter that. He hadn't thought of it that way. "You drink blood?"

"Well done," Leona said while sarcastically clapping her hands. "Yes. But you already knew that. In anticipation of your next question, I feed on people."

"So you're a murderer."

"Yes," she answered simply. "I only go after people who deserve it."

"What do you mean? Who deserves to be murdered?"

"Rapists, other murderers, thieves, pedophiles."

"Not all criminals deserve to die," Sebastian said.

"You're defending rapists? Murderers?"

"No," he said. "I'm saying there's a gray area. I used to be a criminal. Doesn't mean I deserve to get the blood drained from my body."

"What kind of criminal?"

"I stole a lot when I was a kid. Needed money for food. Victor plucked me from a life of crime and helped me turn everything around."

"Believe me, Sebastian, the people I kill deserve to die. I take life very seriously. You either waste it or you don't."

The man huffed. "You take life seriously? You aren't even alive."

Her expression shifted momentarily, then returned to a relaxed state. "No, I'm not. My life was taken from me. I never wanted this. I don't agree with what your friends want. None of us got a choice, but Piper and Whitney are hypocritical when it comes to that. I think my presence just isn't enough for them anymore and they want some new friends," she scoffed.

"You have every right to be afraid. You *should* be. We're your natural predators."

"There's nothing natural about you," Sebastian snapped.

"Ouch," Leona laughed, putting her hand to her chest. "If I had a heart, it would be broken."

He ignored that comment and stayed as far away from her as he could. "So if you're not here to convince me to join your cult, and you're not here to kill me, *once again*... Why. Are. You. Here?"

"Because you intrigue me, Sebastian. Not many humans get to know about us. Or live to tell the tale. I saw you from across the room. I felt drawn to you. That doesn't happen often."

"Drawn to me? No shit. You're drawn to everyone with a pulse. We're all just your next meal," he said. "None of this makes any sense."

"No, it doesn't," Leona said with a sympathetic smile. "But if you can forget that I'm some soulless creature from Hell, perhaps we can be friends."

"Friends," Sebastian said dubiously. "You and your coven want to *kill* my best friends, and you want us to braid each other's hair and spill secrets? Have a sleepover sometime?"

"I told you, I don't want—"

"You waltz here and just... want to take everything away. I don't give a shit what you want, Leona. Apparently you and your friends don't either. You need to stay away from Victor and Charlotte. This is a momentary lapse in judgment on their part."

"They're adults, Sebastian. I don't agree with it, but if

Piper and Whitney want to turn them, I can't stop them. They're old enough to make their own decisions. You don't get to police them."

"You don't even know them," Sebastian snapped.

"I don't have to. That goes for everyone. My choices got taken away from me. I won't do that to someone else who is of sound mind, despite disagreeing with it. This life is suited better to some than others."

Sebastian felt utterly exhausted. He wasn't sure if she was working some kind of vampiric magic on him to influence his mood and demeanor, but he didn't want her here any longer to find out. "Get out of my house."

Leona heaved a sigh and stood up quickly, before flitting over to him in an instant. "Thanks for talking to me. I'm all ears for any more questions."

"Go."

Sebastian stared at the space she left before he could blink again. It felt even colder now than it had when she was here. Had that been some sort of sick power play? He knew damn well she could break into his home and snap his neck without even chipping a nail. He would stand no chance against her. Was it mercy? Surely not.

His head hurt. And he definitely wasn't going back to sleep now.

Later that morning, his house was two blondes fuller. Sebastian sat in an armchair across from them, staring at them intently, waiting for one of them to start.

"Sebastian, I'm sorry," Charlotte said, breaking the silence. He could hear the genuineness in her tone. "We just didn't know how to tell you. We knew you had to see it to believe it."

"Didn't know how to tell me?" Sebastian scoffed. "Didn't know how to tell me you want an assisted suicide from complete strangers? That you want to leave your lives behind — leave *me* behind — for what? An empty promise of immortality? Where did this even come from? Where did you meet them?"

"We met Piper first," Victor chimed in. "Several months ago when we were abroad. In Spain. We got lost and she gave us directions, we offered to buy her dinner and she declined. Charlotte coaxed her into it and we got to talking. She was there visiting a boyfriend. Found out we were from New Orleans and told us she's visited the city many times. Asked if we believed in all the scary stories. I told her where I work, our backgrounds, and our ambitions. I knew there was something different about her. So I outright asked. I think she appreciated my candor and told me what she was. We didn't believe her at first — because it's just so unbelievable. Why would a vampire just tell a human she just met about her abilities? So I assumed she wanted to kill us. Maybe she did. I'll never know," he said. "We offered her money, and then… we offered our blood. In exchange for information. Books don't do this shit justice," he said as he shook his head. "There exists a partnership between some vampires and humans. There's a whole network of leech-like relationships. We offer blood, they don't kill random people. A bond forms between the host and the parasite."

"They hate that word," Charlotte scolded while nudging him.

"Sorry," he mumbled. "The… *passenger*."

"So… you're letting these *things* suck your blood so you can… what, be in with their crowd? Protection from other beings? What?" Sebastian asked, his expression cold, yet curious.

"Yes and no. Among other things," Charlotte said, taking over the conversation. "We became friends with her and Whitney. When we came back here, they would drop in from time to time. We shared correspondence. Kept in touch. We talked about it several times over and decided that we want that lifestyle."

"It's *not* a lifestyle. You aren't just deciding to go off the grid and live in the woods. You're talking about killing yourselves to… what? What's the goal?"

"Think about it, Sebastian. Think about everything they must have seen by now. They're over *three hundred* years old! They have lived through so much history. They have no threats. No fears. They go through their lives and just… do whatever they want. They don't worry about money. They don't worry about petty things like food or housing. They can be whoever they want."

Sebastian rubbed his face in frustration. "You already *have* everything, Charlie. You have everything a person could possibly want. Money, a giant home, a good job, and a husband who loves you. Why throw that away? What's wrong with a long and happy life together?"

"Sebastian," Charlotte sighed sadly. "You just don't understand. This is what we want."

"No!" he boomed, standing up. "No. I don't accept that. I'm not *letting you*—"

"It's not your call," Victor said seriously. He stood up and walked over to him. "I need you to calm down. You're getting worked up."

"Get the hell off me," he snapped, shoving his arm away as he reached out. "Why did you do all that shit for me when we were kids if you were just going to leave me? All alone?"

"This isn't about you, Bas. You know that. You're lashing out," Victor said. "You're scared. You aren't going to lose us. Why do you think we told you? We could have just let you believe we died. We could have let you grieve. We were selfish and asked if we could bring you in. We thought we'd…"

"We thought we'd be able to convince you to do it with us. Be with us forever," Charlotte finished. "If you're so scared of losing us, then—"

"Don't," Sebastian said. "Don't ask me that. You can't *possibly* be asking me that. This is insane," he said, laughing in disbelief. "I feel like I'm in some sort of fever dream," he said, bringing his hands up to his face, his fingers rubbing his eyes.

"Leona said she visited you," Victor said. "She said you had a lot of questions."

"So what?" Sebastian said, turning from him. "I just found out vampires are real. Of course I had questions. Doesn't mean I want to be like you. If anything, I want it even less."

"Well…" Charlotte said, shooting Victor a look. "Maybe

you can come by for dinner this weekend. We won't bother you until then."

Sebastian kept his back to them. "Fine."

Victor started to reach out, but Charlotte pulled him away. They left his house without another word. Sebastian stared down at the deep wood covering his floor, trying to calm himself down. He counted each of the little knots and grains peppering the boards. He lifted his head, his eyes scanning over the bookcases lining the walls of his living room. All the things he'd read, and this was unbelievable to him. All the stories, the fantasies he pored over growing up, and this was something he couldn't wrap his head around. It was laughable.

He felt like he'd wandered into a snake pit.

5

"So, how'd your talk go with tall, dark, and handsome?" Piper asked while eyeing Leona playfully.

They were sitting in Piper's estate, an old French home that she'd bought about a century ago. She came back every few years to make sure it was kept up. She loved this city and loved coming back to it, but she also loved seeing the rest of the world. It wasn't like there was much else to do in her existence. She had a running agreement going with one of her human pets to check in, clean the house, and make sure everything was still functioning normally. He was also good in bed, which never was a bad thing when it came to the blonde.

"It... went," Leona responded, resting her head atop her fingertips. "He hates our kind. He doesn't even *know* about our kind. He also resents us for considering turning Victor and Charlotte."

"Well, that's not up to him," Piper shrugged. "Let him pout. It's their decision. Truly, at the end of the day, it's *ours*. If they don't work out, we can just kill them and be done with it."

"Nice, Pipe," Whitney said, her eyes rolling. "We're not like that anymore."

"It was a joke," Piper groaned. "What else did he say?"

"He asked a lot of questions about us. Sunlight, what we ate, the myths," Leona said. "I answered them all but he still was just as terrified. He *reeked* of fear. I almost felt bad," she sighed.

"I just don't want you to get your heart broken again, Le. You've been through this time and time again with these human men. This one will be no different. Even if he is playing hard to get."

"It's different this time," Leona said, her face hard in thought. "There's something about him."

"Here we go…" Whitney said, tilting her head back.

"Not like that. I mean, truly different. The first time I laid eyes on him, I felt… like I knew him. I can't put my finger on it. He seems so familiar and it puts me on edge."

"Maybe it was just love at first sight," Piper teased, her tongue between her teeth.

"Shut up," Leona snapped. "I can't help but want to be around him. I want to pursue him. But I don't want to scare him away."

"I would say let him come to you, but… with how he responded to you rocking up to his house, I don't know if that's the best plan. Why don't you try to invite him to dinner or something?"

"Well, remember Charlotte told us they invited him this weekend. We should go," Whitney said. "He may not be there, but at least you'll get to know them better, Leona. I think you'll really like them if you give them a chance. They get along famously with us. It's not often we come across good people that could come into our fold."

"Our fold is fine the way it is," Leona said.

"Is it? What if Sebastian suddenly had a change of heart and wanted to join us? What then?"

"Shut up," Leona repeated.

"Sweetheart, listen," Piper sighed, moving to sit beside her on the sofa. She took her hands and squeezed them. "I know you're dealing with a lot of trauma from *him*, but this is supposed to be your escape. You're safe here, he doesn't know where you are. Damien is keeping him at bay. But if word gets 'round that you're fucking some human boy, he *will* come after you. Both of you. If you feel this strongly about this man — who you just met, might I add — then perhaps the best course of action would be to keep your distance. We'll turn his friends, he'll die eventually, and you won't even remember him. Humans tend to get annoyingly… *attached*, and that's not something you need right now. You'd be signing his death warrant."

Leona stared at her sadly. "It's not fair," she whispered. "I didn't *ask* for this. I didn't ask to be like this."

"None of us did. But if you *weren't* like this, you would never have met Sebastian. You'd have been dust under the ground before he was even a passing thought. We aren't meant to mate with humans. It's unnatural and it's part of our curse. The best hope *all* of us have is to stay one step ahead of Gideon," she murmured, then tensed as Leona winced. "Sorry."

"Damien hasn't sent any kind of word to me recently, and that's a good thing," Whitney chimed in, moving to sit on the other side of Leona. "Silence is good when it comes to those men. It means they're busy. I'd prefer they stay that way because it keeps their eyes off us. I think Theodore may come visit soon though. He mentioned it a few weeks ago. You know how he is," she muttered.

"Theo," Piper mumbled disapprovingly under her breath. "If he does decide to come, he needs to find another bed to lie in, because last time he and Damien were here, my place smelled like wet dog for *months*," she grimaced, shaking her head. "Alright, no more talk about those idiots. To say their names is to give them power within this house, which I'll be having none of."

"Agreed," Leona and Whitney said in unison.

They had been inseparable for the last three centuries. Leona was turned before both of them, and met them on her travels in the next couple of years. Leona was, however, the youngest human of the trio, both of them being a few years older than her. She was turned at 20 years old, and would forever look that way.

"Do you think I'm being silly for wanting companionship?" Leona said after an age of silence.

"No," Piper said. "I just think you need to understand that we might be all we've got. And that's not a bad thing to have, darling. It could always be worse and you know it."

Leona looked away from her and stared at the wall, contemplating what she'd said. She *had* experienced worse and didn't want to ever go through that again — despite knowing that it was likely. Perhaps they were right.

These women had completely been her saving grace. Had it not been for their friendship, Leona would have either offed herself or found a way for someone else to do it for her *long* ago. They were the only reason she had escaped from Gideon the two times she had. She thanked everything around her for the relationship Whitney had with Damien, and in turn, the relationship Damien had with Gideon. There was a certain persuasion that existed that *almost* gave Gideon a soft spot when it came to showing mercy on Leona.

Almost.

She knew it was dangerous to feel the things she felt, and the women next to her were right, this wasn't the first time a human had caught her eye. Before, it had been things like a one-night stand or perhaps a short-term boyfriend. Or girlfriend. Everyone was short-term to her, considering she was too afraid to be with any immortals. The feeling was mutual. Gideon had staked his claim within the community that she was off-limits, so any hope for a happily forever after with someone who could actually try to protect her from her creator was dashed away.

There was something so different about Sebastian, though, as she'd told her friends. It wasn't love at first sight, given Leona didn't believe in anything as silly as that. It was more of an inherent recognition, one that would vex her in the days to come. Weeks, even. Looking at him, she felt a pull toward him, and had just wanted to… both run toward him and get as far away from him as possible. He wasn't an immortal, which had been her first momentary thought. She doubted he was a descendant of anyone she'd met before, but then again, she didn't know hardly anything about him. Perhaps he came from a long line of supernatural beings and got the short end of the human stick.

Either way, she wanted to find out. She wanted to know *everything* about him.

6

against his better judgment, Sebastian went to the dinner.

He knew better than to show up to the Labasques under-dressed, no matter how casual the occasion was. Donned in a simple pair of dark jeans, a black sweater, and his black overcoat, he figured this would meet their approval. He doubted much of the attention would be on him anyway. They had better *friends* now.

Sebastian let himself into the house, a delicious aroma beckoning him in. The servants they had were already hard at work. Unease settled in his stomach as he walked through the foyer. There was a shift in the air that he was, regrettably, beginning to get used to. And judging by the unfamiliar voices he heard a few rooms over, his hunch was right.

"Sebby?" Charlotte called out from across the house. "Come back here!"

Sebastian forced himself to walk, though his shoes felt like they were filled with cement. He found Charlotte, Whitney, Piper, Leona, and Victor all gathered in the sunroom, sitting and chatting as if nothing was wrong in the world. As if this was the most normal thing to ever happen, inviting vampires into a home and begging them to kill you.

"Hello," Sebastian said stiffly.

"Did you bring wine?" Victor asked, nodding to the bottle in his hand.

"Yes," he said, looking down. Suddenly, he felt rude for only bringing things that they could enjoy, not the immortals. "I did not bring things suitable for your kind."

"We already ate," Leona said. "We're just here to socialize. I was hoping you'd come," she admitted.

"Sebastian, why don't you take Leona for a tour of the backcourt? I think she'll enjoy it," Charlotte said with a pointed smile.

No arguing there, obviously. Sebastian huffed a quiet breath and decided to get on with things. They weren't going anywhere, evidently, so he might as well make the best of a bad situation. "Okay," he acquiesced. "Is anyone else coming?"

"Just you two," Piper said with a coy smile.

Sebastian found this odd, and his alarm bells were sounding off in his head. His eyes followed the redhead as she stood up, then was by his side in an instant. A shiver crept up his spine and he tried to stave it off. It was odd, looking at her. He didn't want to be rude, because, on the surface, she looked like any other woman. It was going against his moral code to write her off. He felt a pull to her, but he also felt a distinct aversion to her. It was the most intense sense of conflict he'd ever faced in his life.

The two walked outside into the brisk, night air. Things were starting to cool down in Louisiana, which made life so much easier. He supposed she never had to deal with being bothered by any sort of temperature.

He *did* have a lot of questions for her. He'd accepted the fact that if she wanted to kill him, she probably would have done it already. Or was she the type to play with her food? The danger of this situation, of being so close to her, was not lost on him.

"Sorry about all this," Leona said, breaking the silence. "I know you don't want to be doing any of this. I just want to get to know you, Sebastian. I'm not trying to hurt you. I'm not trying to turn you. I told you, I feel drawn to you. I would feel remorseful if I didn't explore that feeling."

"Whether I want it or not, right?" Sebastian mumbled, staring straight ahead.

Leona pulled on his arm and forced him to stop. "You are more than welcome to walk away right now. You didn't have to come to this dinner. You didn't have to let me into your house the other day. You don't have to say one word to me. But you do. You did. Why?"

Sebastian stared down at her. He didn't know how to answer that question, because he'd been avoiding it ever since he met her. "If I had told you to leave — which I *did* — you wouldn't have listened. You would have come in either way. You could snap my neck before I could take my next breath. Denying you the things you want doesn't seem to be in my best interests, Leona."

"I wouldn't do anything you don't want. Tell me you don't want me to be around you anymore and I will listen. I had my choices taken from me. I won't do the same to you. I apologize if I have already."

Sebastian hesitated. Every cell in his being was screaming at him to push her away, tell her that he wanted her to leave, and never deal with any of this again. Something was stopping him though. Perhaps he was drawn to her, too.

At his silence, a slow smile spread across Leona's lips. "We can be friends, then. Is that so bad? I'm not so different from you."

"I've never been friends with such an old woman," Sebastian said, a ghost of a smirk playing around his lips.

Leona's jaw dropped and she scoffed. "You *are* an asshole," she laughed. "I thought gentlemen weren't supposed to comment on a lady's age."

"*You're* a lady?"

Leona grinned and shrugged. "Sometimes. Depends on my mood." She started walking with him again, her arms by her sides. "Do you want to ask me any more questions, Sebastian? I know you have them."

Sebastian stayed at her pace. "I do have them. Far too many of them. So many that we would miss dinner and probably several more dinners after that. But for someone who seems so closed off to everyone else, I'm a bit surprised you want to be so open with me."

"That's what friends do, right?"

"I guess," Sebastian said.

"Why don't you tell me something about you then?

And I'll trade for something about me. We keep going until someone doesn't want to share anything else. That way we're both just as comfortable as the other."

"That seems fair," he said. "Ladies first."

"You *just* insinuated that I was not a lady."

Sebastian did smile at this. "Touché. Fine. I have known Victor since I was a child, and Charlotte for... about a decade now."

"Was that so hard?" Leona said with a smile. "My turn. I have been friends with Piper and Whitney for over three hundred years."

"When you say over..."

Leona laughed. "For me, it's been..." she trailed off, thinking for a moment. "Three-hundred-thirty years now. About three-hundred-ten of being a vampire."

Sebastian's eyebrows shot up to his hairline. "You were born in the sixteen-hundreds?"

She nodded. "Yes. Sixteen-eighty-four. I was turned at twenty years old."

"How did that happen?"

"Hey," Leona said with a smirk. "You owe me at least two details about you. You're getting ahead of yourself."

"Oh," Sebastian said. "Why don't you ask me questions like I have been doing to you?"

"Very well. Are you afraid of me, Sebastian? I'll know if you lie."

"Then why bother asking?"

"Because I want to hear it from you."

Sebastian paused and thought about his answer. She

would know if he lied, and he wasn't a liar to begin with. "Yes," he answered simply.

"For what it's worth, I'm sorry. I don't want to frighten you, but I understand. You *should* be afraid. And I should stop pursuing you, but… I'm selfish."

"Selfish?" Sebastian repeated in confusion. "What is there to be selfish about?"

"Because I'm going against my moral code to be around you. In more than just a predatory way."

"So it *is* predatory."

Leona smirked. "Sort of."

"What is *that* supposed to mean? Are you so cryptic because you're as old as time?"

"Ass," she scoffed. "And we are so uneven in our truth-sharing. You need to start coughing up some secrets."

Sebastian stopped walking and he looked down at her. "Fine. I'll tell you anything you want to know if you answer *one* question truthfully and straight. No riddles, no euphemisms, just direct."

"You really like making bargains, don't you?"

"If you aren't going to play along, we can go back inside. I didn't come out here with you to have idle chit-chat."

"Why *did* you come out here, then, Sebastian?"

"I want to know *right now* what you want with me. Why are you being selfish and why do you keep pursuing me? You told me it wasn't to kill me, so I want to know what you want."

Leona took a step closer to him and raised her eyebrows. "You really want to know?"

"Yes," Sebastian sighed in exasperation. Talking to her

was like talking to a damn Sphinx.

"I want to fuck you."

Silence washed over them as those five words hung in the air. Sebastian opened his mouth to speak, then closed it, then opened it again, then closed it a final time. He searched her eyes, looking for any sign of deceit. It would be quite a wicked prank to play on him, coming from a woman who could literally have whatever she wanted the *moment* she wanted it. He appreciated that she hadn't forced him into anything.

"Why?" was the only thing Sebastian's brain could send to his mouth.

Leona let out a breathy laugh and tilted her head. "So many questions. Why does anyone want to fuck anyone? I'm attracted to you. Is that so hard to believe?"

"Yes," he said honestly. "Women like you — undead or not — don't want to *fuck* men like me."

"And what kind of man are you, Sebastian?"

The man stared down at her, trying to figure both her and her question out. He liked to think he was a good man with a good heart, but that was really for other people to decide. He definitely wasn't the type of man that fucked vampires. Was he?

He could feel a pull between them. The tension was thick and he wasn't sure if she was using some sort of glamour to seduce him or coerce him into giving in. She felt magnetic—

"Hey!" Victor called out from the back door of the manor. "Dinner is ready. Are you two coming in?"

Sebastian jumped slightly at the intrusion and tensed, before looking away from Leona. "Yes, we're coming now," he called out. He walked away from her without looking back.

Sebastian didn't participate much during dinner. He didn't have anything to say, and there was far too much running through his head. Her rather direct and crude statement outside had nearly knocked him off his feet.

He was a red-blooded male. Attraction to her was not the issue. This was a situation he had never found himself in — immortality aside. He'd had a few hookups in his life, nothing long-term. It was always just to scratch an itch. He had never had a *serious* girlfriend before. Being around new people who weren't Charlotte and Victor wasn't easy for him. He had flitted from various odd jobs throughout the city: bookshop clerk, retail associate, and even a bartending stint once. None of that had worked out. He *hated* being around people. He hated speaking to them, interacting with them, and even looking at them. People had never done anything for him his entire life, so the less time he spent around them, the better. This wasn't conducive to life in a city vibrant with tourism and culture, and when his two best friends were some of the biggest socialites in the state. Turning to art had made things much easier. When he photographed the city and sold his prints, or played music, or created paintings, he didn't have to talk to anyone. He could just be with his thoughts in his house in complete silence.

He had gone to college with Victor on an academic scholarship to New York University. It hadn't been his first choice — or any choice — but Sebastian hadn't wanted to be left behind, so off he went up north. Victor had gone to school for business and politics, whereas Sebastian remained undecided with his studies. His scholarships demanded he make a decision and graduate within the four-year period, so he settled on art. He could have stayed in New York for the rest of his life, and he was quite surprised Victor didn't want to. Charlotte had been the pendulum swing for both of them; wherever she went, Victor went, and then Sebastian went. He loved his family with all his heart, and being away from them simply wasn't an option.

Victor also didn't want to be far from him because he 'worried too much,' as he'd told Sebastian once. Though Sebastian refused to accept money from him once he got older, Victor helped him in other ways: job interviews, a roof over his head while Sebastian found his footing, food, and emotional support. There wasn't a doubt in his mind that he'd be dead without Victor.

Leona watched Sebastian closely throughout the meal, trying to gauge his thoughts. She tried not to manipulate minds without permission, given it was really rather rude. She had debated being so direct with him earlier, not wanting to scare him off, but *he* had asked for the truth. The fact that he hadn't run away or simply laughed her off was promising and gave her a little bit of hope. Maybe she could convince him to give her a chance.

"Sebastian, you and Leona should exchange phone numbers. Just in case," Charlotte said with a meddling smile.

"Oh, I don't have a phone—"

"You can have mine," Piper said quickly. "I was going to get a new one anyway," she said, before giving Sebastian the number. "Call her *any* time."

"Okay..." Sebastian muttered, looking down at the new contact in his phone. It seemed like everyone was in on this except him. Had Leona spoken to his friends about her feelings for him? Did they approve? They must, if they were going to this much effort to put them in a room together. Leona didn't even know him, how could she want all this? How could she want *him*?

"Sebastian, don't feel pressured," Leona reassured. "*Please.*"

He shook his head. Nobody could make him do anything he didn't truly want. "I don't."

7

eona stared down at the phone, *willing* something to come through. They had returned home from dinner without discussing much more with Sebastian. She had put enough on his plate as it was. Mentally, she was kicking herself for being so bold with him. It hadn't exactly been the reaction she'd been hoping for. In the past, directly coming on to a man was the way to go, and it had never taken multiple encounters of her practically handing herself over on a silver platter. He was different, and it only ever made her want him more.

"Still waiting?"

Leona looked up at the blonde hovering in the doorway. She shifted from where she was lounging in her nook by the window. "Yes."

"Leona," Piper sighed, walking over to her. She perched down on the edge of the windowsill and placed a hand on the redhead's knee. "I know you fancy Sebastian. He seems nice.

But I'm not sure this is the best idea. You're already getting too attached and you haven't so much as hugged yet. You know love is a tricky thing for beings like us."

"You're such a hypocrite, Piper," Leona snapped.

"Excuse me?" she scoffed. "What the hell have I done?"

"Who was it that practically threw this phone across the dinner table *fawning* over Sebastian and me exchanging numbers? Who was it that plotted with those humans to send us both outside to 'take a tour?'"

Piper pressed her lips together in a thin line, not having a retort. "I want you to be happy, Le, but I don't know if this is the best way to go about it. I thought, perhaps… but he hasn't reached out. Maybe you just have to accept that he's not interested."

Leona frowned and rested her head against the windowpane, her pale features illuminated by the moonlight. "It's not fair, Pipe."

"I know it's not," Piper said. She scooted closer to her and gently embraced her. "Humans and our kind just… don't mix. You know that."

"Well, our kind and *I* don't mix. As long as Gideon—"

"*Don't.*"

"As long as *he's* around, I can't mate with a vampire anyway. He would destroy them. No human stands a chance against him either. I'm doomed to either spend the rest of my existence running away or give in to his abuse and be a slave. I'd rather *die* than go back to his prison."

"You will never have to go back," Piper said seriously. "That's why you have us. We protect each other. He has kept his distance and Theodore and Damien are ensuring it stays that way for the time being. He won't stay away forever, but... for now, that's what we've got."

"Sebastian isn't like him."

"You don't know that. You don't know that human. He's a man, they're all the same. That's why we stay one step ahead."

"I told him I wanted to fuck him. He hardly flinched. In fact, he looked *frightened* by that. Shocked, even."

Piper barked out a laugh. "No shit. He probably is frightened. Probably thinks you'll throw him through the bed frame."

"That was *one* time—"

"Still," she smirked. "Just because he didn't strip down starkers doesn't mean he didn't want to love you and leave you. You *know* how humans are. They are intrigued, then they get in over their heads, get scared, try to run away, and *we* have to clean up *your* mess. I am *really* trying to keep my track record of killing innocent humans clean. I don't want to live that way anymore."

"Neither do I," Leona said sadly. "I just want to be normal. I want to fall in love and have babies—"

"Leona."

"What?!" she cried out, snapping her head over to her. "I *know* it can't happen, but I can dream, can't I? Why shouldn't I be able to find a man who loves *me*? Who doesn't want me for immortality or money. Or to stroke his ego and show off his power. I want a man who's content to sit here and read a book with me. Or who will give me flowers just because it's a Tuesday and not because he wants something in return.

I want a *gentleman*. I thought Gideon was a gentleman..." she trailed off quietly, cutting her eyes down. "Sometimes I wonder if I'd be better off dead."

"Stop thinking that way," Piper said firmly. "You *can't* think that way. He will win if you do. I know you're sad, but this will pass. It always does. You just need a good, hard shag."

"Ugh," Leona grimaced, shaking her head. She thunked her temple next to the glass pane again. "The thought of bedding another random man makes me want to vomit. If I could."

The phone lying in front of them on the cushion they were atop lit up and Piper picked it up. A small smile spread across her lips and she held it out to Leona. "Maybe you won't have to."

The redhead looked down at the phone and instantly sat up straight at the name above the notification. It was one word, one simple *Hi*. It was enough to make the still heart in her chest skip a beat.

"Get out," Leona then gasped, nudging her away.

"What?!" Piper laughed, standing up with a slight stumble. "No way. I want to see what he says!"

"No!" Leona snapped. "Get *out*."

"Fine, fine. I'll know if you sneak out tonight, just saying," she called out as she left the room, the door shutting behind her.

Leona took a deep breath, more for herself than anything, and crossed her legs. She opened the phone and stared down at the thread Sebastian had started. One little grey bubble with one little word. She had to get this right.

> Hi.
> It's Sebastian.

> > I know. I'm glad you reached out. I was just thinking about you.

> Good thoughts, I hope.

> > Extremely. What are you doing?

> I'm sitting on my back porch with a beer. Texting you. Wondering if this is a bad idea.

> > Let me know when you make a decision. Maybe I can sway you a little bit.

> Do you do this a lot?

> > Do what? Text? This is my first time.

> No. Flirt with guys. This whole charade. Do you usually go to so much effort to sleep with someone? Why not just take whatever you want? It's not like someone could stop you.

> > That's not the kind of person I am. Things were different in my time. Not so forward.

> I see.

> > Can I call you?

Leona watched the small bubble filled with three dots pop up, disappear, pop up, then disappear. What did that mean? Why did it go away? Did he not—

Buzz — Buzz — Buzz.

Her eyes widened as she saw his name pop up big on the screen. She slowly slid the button across and put the phone up to her ear. "Hello."

"Hi again."

"For a second I thought you weren't going to respond."

"I hate waiting for other people to call me, so I decided to take the initiative after your question. I'll admit this is much easier than texting."

"I agree. But we can continue our conversation. Did you decide whether this is a good idea or not?"

"Jury's still out. But maybe telling me more about what 'your time' was like will help me make a decision."

Leona smiled. "What do you want to know, Sebastian?"

"What year were you born again?"

"Sixteen-eighty-four."

"When did you become a vampire?"

"I already told you all this."

"Tell me again. I can make notes now."

"You're writing this down?"

"Trying to. If you'd answer the question, I could start."

Leona smiled. "I was turned when I was twenty. Just before my wedding."

"You were going to be married?"

"Yes. But then I wasn't. He wasn't what I thought he was. I was young, naive, and stupid. I was in love with the idea of love. I wanted the things everyone talked about with that dreamy look in their eyes. Gideon noticed that and pounced. My family was all too eager to have this nice, posh bachelor set his sights on me. My father was happy to let him take me away. I was, too. He courted me for two and a half years before he proposed. We planned the wedding for a year and a half. For nothing, I might add. I still wonder why he was so patient, but... that amount of time is a mere blink for an immortal. I suppose it was all just amusement for him."

"So... Gideon is your creator?"

"Yes."

"And... where is he now?"

"As far away as possible, I hope. He has an estate in England, in the country. He likes his privacy. I assume he's there or just wandering somewhere else in the world, finding people to prey on."

"What happened that made you hate him so much?"

"He's a monster, Sebastian," Leona simply said, letting those words marinate between them.

After an age, Sebastian broke the silence. "I'm sorry."

Leona laughed quietly on the other end. "Thank you. It's not an enjoyable story to tell. But if you want to hear it, I'll continue."

"Maybe you can tell me when we're face-to-face. Doesn't seem like the kind of story fit for a phone call. Or maybe a *really* long text."

She giggled, a smile permanently fixed on her face. "Hearing that I have some scary, powerful, ancient vampire ex-boyfriend doesn't intimidate you even a *little* bit?"

"Well... how tall is he?"

"Probably close to seven feet."

"Shit."

Leona laughed harder, covering her mouth. "He has red eyes, too."

"Shitter shit."

"Short hair."

"Abs?"

"We all have abs."

"*There's* a selling point," he teased.

"Shut up. I'm sure you already have abs."

"Only one way to find out."

If she could blush, she would have. "If I didn't know better, I'd think you're flirting with me, Sebastian Beliveau."

"Good thing you don't know better. Maybe your brain is rotting with age. Along with everything else."

"Asshole," she said, with no malice in her tone. But she heard him laughing on the other end. "When do I get to see you again?"

"I'm trying to play hard to get. I've heard girls love that."

"I'm more of an instant gratification girl myself."

"Spoiled. The word for that is spoiled. Spoiled brat, by extension."

"And the word for you, again, is *asshole*."

"Thank you," he cooed.

Leona's smile widened and it took everything in her not to kick her feet with excitement. She stood up and began to pace. "You never answered my question. When do I get to see you again?"

"People will start to talk…"

"Let them," Leona groaned. "Sebastian!"

"I have a few photoshoots tomorrow. One is at sunset. We

can meet afterward. Is that dark enough?"

"Yes," she said, relief flooding through her. "Tomorrow after sunset. Where?"

"By the river?" he suggested. "Across from the Cathedral."

"It's a date."

"Is it?"

Leona paused. "Can it be?"

Now it was Sebastian's turn to pause. She was about to scrap everything and laugh it off when his deep voice rumbled from the other line, "A first date with you calls for much more than a walk along the river. I promise you, if you and I go on a date, you'll know about it."

Leona released a short breath. How lovely. Nobody had ever said anything so gentle and sweet to her before, which made her rather sad. Were her standards really so low?

"That sounds perfect, Sebastian. I'm excited to see you."

"Likewise," he said. "I should let you get to sleep."

"Did I tell you I was immortal? I was sure it had come up…"

"You don't sleep? What about coffins?"

Leona made a face to herself. "*Ghastly*."

Sebastian chuckled to himself. "No sleep at all?"

"We *can* sleep, but it's not a true sleep. More just resting our eyes. We're always *awake*. It's difficult to explain."

"What the hell do you do all day and night then?"

"Read. Things got much easier when the telly was invented. And now there's the Internet."

"Lots of porn, huh?"

"*Sebastian*," she hissed. "I may be immortal *and* lonely, but I am still a woman of integrity. Don't be so crass."

"Sorry, m'lady," he teased. She could *hear* his smirk. "Fine. *I'll* go to sleep. I actually need it. This isn't natural beauty, you know."

"You *are* beautiful, Sebastian. Inside and out."

That caught Sebastian off guard. He stayed quiet for several moments, then he shifted in his seat. "I'll see you tomorrow, Leona."

"Goodnight, Sebastian."

"Goodnight."

Leona pressed the red button to end the call, then she held the phone against her chest. She felt like crying. She settled back into her reading nook and looked out into the night scenery, taking it all in. She had learned to fall in love with the dark. But she did miss the light.

For the first time in a few centuries, she felt happy.

8

$\mathfrak{A}$s Sebastian plugged in his phone and got ready to turn in for the night, he heard movement from the front of his home. Sitting up, he reached over to his nightstand cautiously, his ears straining to hear. Had he been imagining things? For a moment, he wondered if it was Leona, but quickly squashed that possibility. They had just agreed to meet each other another time. Her friends, perhaps? Even more unlikely.

Before he could get his weapon out of the drawer beside him, a figure's platinum hair shone through the darkness. Sebastian grunted and slumped in relief, before shaking his head. "Charlotte! You almost got stabbed."

"You're so dramatic," the blonde scoffed as she turned on the light, causing Sebastian to wince and blink a few times. "What are you doing?"

"What am I doing? What are you doing?! It's nearly one in the morning and you have broken into my house."

"Again, dramatic. It's not breaking in if you have a key, we've been over this. Besides, I'm getting used to my new future life. If I don't get to enjoy the sunlight anymore, I want to try to get used to nightlife. It's rather pretty, you know. Quiet, the stars are visible when the pollution isn't heavy in the sky, and the moonlight shines so beautifully on foggy nights in the Quarter."

Sebastian huffed and tried to ignore everything she was saying. Why was she treating this as if she was going on some fancy vacation abroad? This was a permanent vacation, from literal human life. He, of all people, understood the urge to say 'fuck it' to being alive in the hellhole they called Earth, but to do it for the rest of eternity? And you couldn't even eat pizza anymore? Why the hell would he want to do that? Why would anyone want to do that?

As much as he was warming up to Leona, it didn't mean he wanted to uproot his entire lifestyle to become some creature. It was still even surreal to wrap his head around the fact that this was real.

"I'm tired, Charlie. I'm sure whatever you're here to tell me or do could have been accomplished in a text message or phone call," Sebastian groaned, lying down against the pillows. He pulled the covers over him to try and shield his eyes from the harsh light. "That's your cue to leave."

"Come on," Charlotte said. After a moment, Sebastian felt a dip beside him and knew any further complaints or requests for her to leave would be fruitless.

"Okay, fine. Fine. What do you want? Make it quick, if possible. Some of us aren't practicing being undead."

"I just wanted to talk to you. About everything. Have you even had a real conversation with Vic about this?"

"What is there to say, Charlie?" he asked, pulling the covers down from his face. He stared at her and wondered how different she would be if and when she actually went through with this transformation. Would her eyes still be the same? Her smile? Her kind-hearted yet fierce nature? Would she want to kill him? Would she change from the woman he'd grown to love so hard he'd take a bullet for her?

"He's upset that you're upset. We both care about you, Sebby. That hasn't changed, nor will it ever. I hope you know that. I know you don't understand, but your support would mean the world to us. We don't want to live without you. He's worried about you."

"Worried about me? What about himself? You?"

"There's nothing you can say that will change our minds, Sebastian. I know it doesn't make sense. I know you don't agree. I know it's scary. But I want you to listen to what I'm saying: we aren't going anywhere. We will be here with you always. Just like we promised. Okay?"

"I'm not a child," Sebastian muttered. "You don't have to do this with me, you know."

"I never said you were a child. But your panic attacks get worse when a major change happens. You did this when your parents died. You did it when we were talking about moving away from New York. You try to shut us out and it only makes things worse. You promised last time that if this happened again, you would listen to me and talk to me. Remember what your therapist said?"

"I haven't been to therapy in years."

"Exactly. You don't know how to cope. I can't force you to get the help you need, but I can at least try and give it to you myself. What are you feeling? You can yell, you can break something, you can storm out of the room. I just want to hear what you're thinking. You're always so enigmatic."

Sebastian blinked a few times, feeling his chest grow tight. This was not something he was prepared to address or talk about, especially with her. He should have expected it though. He had been ghosting Victor's texts and calls and was rather surprised he hadn't shown up out of the blue like his wife had. Charlotte was always the more... forward one of them all.

"It feels like you're leaving me," Sebastian eventually murmured.

Charlotte's eyebrows stitched together in concern and she slipped her hand into his, their fingers intertwining. "Why does it feel like that, Sebby?"

"Because..." Sebastian started, feeling frustrated that his thoughts were all over the place. Usually, he was calm, cool, and collected, but currently, he felt like a fog was suffocating every part of his brain that strung together intelligent, well-rehearsed sentences. "You're going to become these... these things. You're getting a new family. One that has powers. One that's unbelievably beautiful. They have seen so much, been through so much, and are all around much more interesting than anyone we've ever met. You're going to be part of their world. And I'm going to be here. The human. The only human."

Charlotte listened to him, letting him get it all out before she responded. Using her free hand, she gently stroked some of his dark waves away from his face, then settled her palm against his cheek. "You're my best human. You always have been. You say you'd be lost without us... We'd be lost without you. You bring so much light to our lives, Sebastian. Anyone is lucky to be in your presence. I know you don't believe me, but... I wish you did. I wish there was a way I could convince you how wonderful you are," she said, searching his eyes. "You are completely unforgettable. There is not a scenario in any universe where you, Victor, and I don't find each other. We are linked forever."

"We won't be. I'll die. You'll continue living. You get forever. I get a few more decades."

"Hopefully more than a few," Charlotte teased gently, a pretty, soft smile spreading across her lips. She gently stroked Sebastian's cheek with her thumb, wanting to soothe any worries he had. "Do you hate us, Sebby?"

The man hesitated, thinking about that question. His brain couldn't even compute that emotion about the Labasques. "I could never."

"Good," Charlotte said. Sliding her hands from his hand and cheek, she snaked her arms around his shoulders and pulled him in close for a hug. Her eyes fluttered shut and she merely breathed him in. She felt his grip tighten on her, like a vice, and she felt his body shudder ever so slightly against her. Not wanting to draw attention to his emotions — something she knew he had trouble experiencing — she merely held him until he caught his breath. "Tell me what you're thinking," she eventually whispered against his hair.

"I was thinking about Mom. Losing her."

Charlotte's throat grew small and she nodded. "I know, honey. This isn't going to be like that, though. Do you hear me?" she asked, pulling back just enough so they could come face-to-face. She wiped his damp cheeks, then held him there. "We got through that. Together. We got through New York and school together. We got through moving here together. That's what we do, Sebby. That's what you and Victor have always done. We would never let anything bad happen to you."

"Okay," Sebastian whispered. He did feel like a child. Their child. Even though they were all within a couple of years of age of each other.

"I'm still sensing some worries in that big brain of yours," Charlotte said, wiping more tears from his cheeks. "Anything else?"

"You know you're going to have to kill people. When you become like them."

Charlotte slowly moved her hands from his face, dropping them in her lap. "Yes."

"You have never done that before."

"Obviously."

"I have."

Charlotte frowned and shook her head. "That was different, Sebastian, and you know it. That bastard deserved what he got. You were avenging your mom. I told you not to blame yourself for that anymore."

"Doesn't matter the circumstances. I still killed him,

Charlie. I took someone's life, even if that someone was evil. I will deal with that for the rest of my days. I still have nightmares about that terrible night. Are you ready to do that over and over again?"

The blonde processed that information. That night — that time — had truly been horrendous. Even she and Victor carried trauma from it. It had been messy, both literally and figuratively, and had been extremely costly in every sense of the word. She was glad it was well behind them.

"It's something I've thought about a hundred times, Bas. You know better than anyone that some people shouldn't be on this planet. Your father was one of them. You know that. He deserved what he got. I just hate that it had to be you."

Sebastian agreed with her. Of course he did. He hated his father and hadn't shed a tear over him. He hadn't even had a funeral for him. His mother was a different story. Even though she wasn't the most present parental figure in the world, she tried. He saw it then and he saw it even more now as an adult who was used to life without her. Sebastian had always felt the urge to protect her because she was unable to do so herself. But life was cruel, and no matter how hard he tried, it hadn't been enough. She died scared and in a horrifically brutal way. There had been countless nights where he lay awake wondering what he could have done differently that would have kept her alive. He just hoped she hadn't felt pain past a millisecond.

"Do you want to come back to the house with me? Stay over? Victor will be so happy," Charlotte suggested, her voice laden with hope.

"No," Sebastian answered, before he could change his mind. "I'll come by tomorrow though. I'll talk to him."

The woman smiled and leaned forward to kiss his forehead. "My Sebby."

"Enough," he groaned, shaking his head away from her. "Do you need me to order you a ride home?"

"Well... I walked here."

"You walked here?!"

"It's not that far."

"It's the middle of the night! You know better," Sebastian snapped. "Anything could have happened to you. There are all sorts of crazy fuckers lurking on the streets at night."

"I know this city well, Bas, and it's barely half a mile."

"All it takes is one second and you're gone. Or worse. I don't even want to think about that..."

"If you're so worried, you can always walk me home."

Sebastian narrowed his eyes and all but glared at her. "I hate you, you know."

The blonde beamed and sprung from the bed. "My big strong protector."

"Shut up," Sebastian muttered, yanking the covers off him. He stood and pulled on some jeans over his boxers, then grabbed a hoodie.

"You might as well just stay the—"

"I know the drill," Sebastian interrupted, grabbing his phone. "Come on, damsel in distress. Let's go."

9

"Oh good. It worked."

Sebastian walked into the manor and snapped his head at his blonde best friend. "What worked?" he asked, then pointedly looked to Charlotte. "Oh, you're a bitch. Both of you, actually."

"I was desperate!" Victor said as he put his hands up in defeat. "I don't like it when you're mad at me. It happens so rarely that I forget what it feels like when it does happen. I hated it."

"So you sent your wife after me?" Sebastian whined, shaking his head. "Evil."

"Drama queen," Charlotte cooed, nudging his shoulder with her hand as she flounced past him. "You know you can't say no to me."

"Shut up," Sebastian snapped. Was he really that angry or annoyed? No. They knew him inside and out, and this happened all the time, whether it be during a fight or even whenever they were trying to surprise him for his birthday.

Which he despised. Every. Time.

"Are you staying the night?" Victor asked, looking him up and down, seemingly for some kind of bag.

"Do I have a choice?" Sebastian said with a great sigh, as if it was the most inconvenient thing in the world. It wasn't. Maybe Charlotte was right. Ugh.

"Well, it's late and I am just exhausted," Charlotte said while putting her hand over her yawn. Sebastian barely managed not to roll his eyes at her poor acting skills. She was the queen of all drama queens. "I'll leave you boys to it. Play nicely," she said, pointing at both of them. "See you in the morning. I'll order breakfast for us."

The men watched her disappear up the stairs, and Sebastian turned to meet Victor's gaze. "Are you going to give me the same heart-to-heart Charlie did? Because I'd really rather not dredge back up my dead parents again while brooding over your imminent doom."

"There is almost never a situation where I want to bring up your parents," Victor said. His joking expression faded, and he placed his hands on his friend's shoulders. "I'm sorry, Bas. I never wanted to hurt you. I know I did though. I hope Charlie was able to convey our feelings on this matter. It's…"

"Complicated. I know," Sebastian said. He was tired of hearing about it, quite frankly. Maybe he was just tired in general.

"I'm glad you came over."

"Me, too."

Victor pulled Sebastian in for a hug, which made

Sebastian tense ever so slightly, before he relaxed. Physical affection was difficult for him. It always had been. Growing up, he had craved love and attention and acceptance, given he never got it from anyone who wasn't trying to exploit him for some reason. Victor and Charlotte were both extremely affectionate and had nearly killed him on several occasions from their hugs, kisses, hair-strokes, or any other unnecessary touch that Sebastian wanted to rip his skin off after. He had gotten used to it over the years, but sometimes it still caught him off guard. Victor also wasn't completely off the hook as far as Sebastian was concerned. Charlotte knew how to work him to her advantage though.

"Want a nightcap? A friend of Father's sent me this aged bourbon. Apparently it was stored and aged below sea level for a decade."

"You are so gullible," Sebastian said with a light smirk, unable to help himself. He melted around these two. Every time. "Come on. I'll try your ocean whiskey."

They walked to Victor's study, which was lined with books that Sebastian was positive were just for decoration. There was no way he had read any of these. It did look nice, he had to admit.

Victor went into a small cupboard and unlocked it with a combination code. Fishing around, he finally pulled out a fancy-looking bottle with ornate designs throughout the glass. Sebastian raised his eyebrows. That did look like something that came from Atlantis.

As they nursed their glasses, Sebastian distracted himself by reading the spines of all the books against the wall for the hundredth time.

"How are you doing, Bas?"

"Don't start this with me, Vic. It's, like, three in the morning."

"I'm serious. This is a lot. Are you taking your medication still?"

"Yes, Daddy," Sebastian drawled, rolling his eyes. He knew it came from a good place, but they did treat him like their child more often than not. He'd rather be treated like a brother.

"You don't have to be like that. If you're upset, tell me. I want to hear it. You spent a long time with Charlie talking to her, so give me the same courtesy."

Sebastian clenched his jaw, then looked at him. "Fine. I'll tell you what I told Charlotte. I'm worried about both of you. You're going to have to kill people to survive. You're going to have to take life. Do you think you'll even enjoy being alive for that long? Surely at some point, you'll have done everything."

"Sebastian, think about it. You get to live forever. You don't have to worry about trivial things like grocery shopping or waking up for work. We already have enough money to last an eternity. This life isn't for us. We want to see the world, meet immortals like them, be part of a new universe. There are so many things we can't even fathom when it comes to their way of life."

"You don't know that. You're romanticizing it. What about a family?"

"You know Charlie can't have kids."

"Birthing a child isn't the only kind of family you can

have. You could adopt. You could get operations to try to make a pregnancy stick. There are options. Is that why you're doing this?"

"No. Not the only reason, anyway," Victor said. "Aren't you even a little curious about the unknown?"

"No," Sebastian scoffed. "It's unknown for a reason, Vic. You don't see me clambering into a rocket ship because I don't understand exactly what a black hole is and want to fly into it. If you're so curious, just read a book. Or two. Or three. There are multiple famous vampire novel authors who live within a ten-mile radius. Go pick their brains. Maybe they're vampires too."

"You don't have to be a dick about it," Victor said with an unimpressed look. "I'm not going to explain or defend this decision anymore. It is our choice, Sebastian. Not yours. I know you're worried about us leaving, but I assure you, that won't happen. We're here for you. I promised you."

"You sound like Charlie," he said, cutting his eyes away from him. "What if this new life changes you? More than just physically. What if I lose you, Vic? The best parts of you. The parts that memorize the lyrics of a song I show you once, or that pick up a record that I mentioned wanting just because, or that save me from killing myself? All the shit I've forced you to endure over the years. I'm just… I can't even make it up to you. I'll never be able to. This is me trying."

"Bas," Victor said, putting his empty glass down on the table nearby. Closing the distance between them, his hands wrapped around Sebastian's elbows. "I'll say it a million more times if you need it: I'm not going to throw you away. I will never tire of you."

Sebastian looked into his eyes, feeling his genuineness. His shoulders relaxed marginally, and after a few breaths, he nodded. "Okay."

"Now this is the part where you say you'll never tire of me and I'm the best thing that ever happened to you," Victor smirked, laughing as Sebastian shrugged him away. "Come on. You and I have never been able to fight for more than, what, three days?"

"Three and a half, technically. When you ate my pasta in the fridge in high school."

"Oh my God," Victor groaned, tilting his head back. "You are never going to get over that, are you? Once again, how was I supposed to know that was yours? Your name wasn't on it."

"Once again, I told you when I put it up the night before that I was already looking forward to eating it when we got home from school. You knew," Sebastian hissed, poking him in the chest.

"Was it really three and a half days?" Victor said with a big smile. Laughter bubbled from within at Sebastian's nod and the blonde ran a hand through his hair, his pale cheeks rosy from the alcohol and his amusement. "How on earth did we not kill each other growing up?"

"It wasn't for lack of trying some days," Sebastian smirked. "Though... dying by a vampire would arguably be the coolest way to go. I'll give you that."

"See? Now you're talking. I knew I could count on you to see the joy in our demise. Your depression really does work wonders for everyone involved."

Sebastian's cheeks hurt from laughing. The alcohol had relaxed him, and he was starting to venture into delirious territory from his lack of sleep, but he did feel better that he and Victor had made up. The issue wasn't exactly resolved, but... Sebastian could table it for another day, hopefully at a better hour.

"I need to go to bed," the dark-haired man said, putting his glass down. "My bed."

"Why are you in such a hurry? You got a photoshoot or something in the morning?"

"In the evening, but..."

"But what?"

"I just want to be well-rested. That's all."

"You are the worst liar."

"I'm not lying!"

"Okay, you're the worst 'omitting-the-truther.' Spill. Hot date?"

"I wouldn't call it a date…"

Victor's face lit up. "No shit. No way is it Leona. Is it?!"

Sebastian made a noise of displeasure and blushed darkly. "It's not a date. We're just going to meet up and talk. Get to know each other. No need to submit an article to the paper."

"Wow. Good for you," Victor said, clapping him on the back. "You want a real good night's rest because you're going to be up all night again tomorrow, hmm?"

"No," Sebastian said, walking past him and to the door. "Is that all you think about?"

"You don't?"

"I mean, not all the time but... Shut up. It's not a date. Just two friends talking. Like me and you."

"You wish," Victor teased.

"Goodnight," Sebastian snapped, leaving the room to go upstairs to his area. Walking back home would be pointless, and honestly, he didn't feel like it. He also didn't feel like dealing with Charlotte's wrath should she wake up and he be gone. He picked his battles when it came to that woman.

10

Surprising himself, Sebastian was looking forward to seeing Leona. He was also in a good mood because his photoshoots had ensured he would make rent *and* eat this week. As much as he hated not having a reliable income, the busy months were good and he could be his own boss. Making his own schedule was worth its weight in gold. And as much as the slow months were slow, things always evened out in the end. He had been thinking about their phone conversation a lot, wondering if he should just let this go. He had never received such attention before, and from someone so interesting. Despite her frightening him, he was beginning to trust her. It didn't make sense to him that she would play with him this long if she wanted to kill him. That she would befriend his best friends just to blow everything up. Surely if she killed him, Charlotte and Victor wouldn't want to join their group.

She had also opened up to him when she didn't have to. If

that wasn't to build trust, what was it?

The river shimmered in the moonlit sky, the lights from nearby ships passing by reflecting off its surface. He often liked to just walk along the bank, letting the breeze wash over him. The hum of the French Quarter was filling his veins, as it always did. It was always split into two halves at night: one side bustling with people partying or drowning their sorrows in alcohol, and the other with people like him who enjoyed the peace with the serenity of the water.

The air around him shifted and he no longer felt alone. Slowly, he turned around, ignoring the jolt within him as he came face to face with those increasingly familiar, piercing green eyes. "Hi."

"Hi," Leona said with a smile. She was wearing a red cocktail dress that shimmered in the dim light, some short, white kitten heels, and her hair was tied up in a bunch of pretty braids atop her head.

She took his breath away.

"You there?" she laughed, moving in front of him a bit.

"Sorry," Sebastian said. "I feel underdressed." He glanced down at his outfit: dark jeans, some Doc Marten boots, and a thin, black, long-sleeve t-shirt. His camera bag was strapped on his back. He looked like he was about to go on some gothic hike.

"Nonsense," she said, waving her hand dismissively. "You just got off work. I wouldn't expect you to run around taking pictures in a full suit. I like dressing like this," she said. "I know you said it wasn't a date. Me dressing nice doesn't make it so. I promise."

He had been grappling with the idea of this technically being a date. It bothered him that he *wanted* it to be. It bothered him that he was starting to expect her presence, miss it even.

"Shall we walk?" he asked, offering his arm.

Leona smiled bashfully and took it. She fell into step beside him and peered out toward the body of water to their left. "It has been a long time since I've merely gone on a stroll."

"You have been to this city before, haven't you?" Sebastian asked, looking over at her.

"Oh, yes," Leona nodded. "More times than I can count. Piper has had a home here for a while now. We always come back eventually. She, Whitney, and I are all from England. Varying parts. When we left the country, we came here. It was the only city really established at the time. We came before the United States was officially a country. It was fun," she admitted. "It had just been established by the French. It was still called La Nouvelle-Orléans. It's come so far."

"Does it look a lot different?"

"Absolutely. You know of the Great New Orleans Fire of seventeen-eighty-eight?" At his nod, she continued. "There are stories on different reasons for it starting, but... truthfully, they found out vampires had infiltrated the city. We were staying in a home, minding our business, and the fires broke out, trying to kill us. Or at least push us out of the city. It was awful," she sighed. "We left for a while. Then we came back a few years later, that's when the Great New Orleans Fire of seventeen-ninety-four happened. We stayed away for even longer after that. Almost a century. We flitted from place to place. But when we thought it was safe, we came back and put roots down. Piper bought the house we're in now and we stayed a long time. Until Gideon found me. He dragged me back. I escaped after a few decades. He hasn't bothered me in…" she paused. "About fifteen years."

"That's great," Sebastian exclaimed. "Do you think he's finally left you alone for good?"

Leona laughed sadly and shook her head, her gaze downward cast at their feet walking in sync. "No. He's left me alone for longer. I'm sure he knows exactly where I am, what I'm doing. He thinks it's all a game. I'm free because he *allows* it. And when he wants me back in his bed, he thinks he can just snap his fingers and snatch me up again. It's maddening."

Sebastian frowned. "Why doesn't anyone *stop* him?"

"Because everyone is afraid of him. Anyone who has tried to stand up to him hasn't survived. He's been around so long that nobody even knows where he came from. Or his exact age."

"If you had to guess…"

"A few thousand. More than three, I'd say. The earliest I've heard him speak about is the Great Pyramids. He wasn't there when they were built, but… he said he visited not long after. But he has never given me an exact date. He has never told me how he was turned. He never told me how his creator died — if they died — and what happened after he became immortal. Looking back, I have no idea how he convinced me to fall in love with him. I was so stupid."

"You were young. You couldn't have known he was a vampire trying to corrupt you."

"I suppose you're right," she said. It didn't stop her from kicking herself sometimes.

"What happened when he dragged you back?"

"He would just make me miserable. He'd control me, lock me away sometimes for years as punishment. He'd make me drink rats and other rodents. He gets off on torture. He loves power. But… it's different with me than others. He has killed vampires he's created. He keeps me around for some reason. He becomes *obsessive*. Territorial, even though I am not his to protect. I have tried to escape him, be with other people — both human and immortal — and move on, but he won't allow it. Any time he finds out I'm with someone, he kills them. Eventually."

Sebastian's eyes were wide. He blushed darkly and continued looking ahead. Leona seemed to realize what she'd said and he could feel her apology bubbling from her throat. Before she could speak, he looked over at her, "You're *really* selling this whole relationship thing well, you know?"

Leona laughed awkwardly and brought a hand up to rub her forehead. "Sorry. I told you I was being selfish by pursuing you."

"Why do you keep doing this to yourself? If he's killed everyone that isn't him, and purposefully makes you miserable, why do you put yourself through it?"

"Because I want to find love, Sebastian. I have never felt true love before. I *want* that. I want as normal a life as I can lead. Is that such a crime?" she asked quietly. She hated feeling like she was being too much just by asking for the bare minimum. "I didn't ask for this life. But this is the life I have, and I want to make the most of it. Nobody should be trapped in a cage. And the rest of eternity is a long time to do so."

Sebastian resisted the urge to reach out to her. He put his hands in his pockets instead. "Have you ever considered killing yourself? Can vampires be killed?"

Leona swallowed thickly and looked over at him, her eyes distant and sad. "Yes, they can. And yes, I have. He wouldn't allow it. He has always found a way to stop it. Piper and Whitney each have stopped it before, too. It's not as easy as it is for humans, and we don't have many options. Oftentimes, another vampire has to do it. When immortals find out I am Gideon's creation, most of them want nothing to do with my plan. Piper and Whitney obviously stopped it because they're my friends, but… they don't truly understand the fear I live with every day. He doesn't have the same hold over them."

Sebastian looked at her, sadness pricking his eyes. He understood her feelings. He didn't have an evil overlord pursuing him, but he had been low many times in his life. He had tried to end things, and his friends had saved him. He owed them his life several times over. It made him all the more bitter that they went through the trouble to save him, and were now throwing their lives away like they were nothing more than yesterday's paper.

"He isn't going to hurt you again."

Leona stopped and looked over at Sebastian. "What?"

The man stopped and searched her eyes. Shaking his head, he repeated, "He isn't going to hurt you again. I won't let him."

"Sebastian… this story ends the same every time."

"You didn't have me the other times."

She smiled, but it didn't reach her eyes. She reached out, gently placing her hand on his cheek. It was hard to ignore how he flinched, ever so slightly. She didn't know if it was due to her cold temperature or if he was just afraid of her touch. It pleased her to see him relax marginally. "You're right. I didn't have you. I wish I had."

Sebastian felt his heart rate quicken. Could she hear it? *Feel* it? He felt connected to her in a way he had never experienced before. "I'm not going to let him touch you," he whispered. "*Ever.*"

Tears burned Leona's eyes and she merely nodded. Her gaze cut downward and she dropped her hand back down to her side. "Thank you," she murmured.

Looking at her reminded Sebastian of his own mother. Of *himself.* He knew the feeling of being imprisoned in your own home. His own father had been a beast of a man. He drank himself into a stupor every other day and turned his anger and hatred for himself on his wife and only son. Ever since he was young, he watched his once vibrant mother turn into a shell of a woman, relying on self-medication to get through her abysmal life. He would not let Leona be broken the same way.

"Sorry I made you cry," Sebastian said sheepishly.

Leona dabbed at her cheeks and let out a breathy laugh. "No, Sebastian, don't be silly. You have nothing to apologize for. I just... wish I could be as selfless as you. We'd both probably be better off for it."

Sebastian shook his head. "You've spent the last three

hundred years being forced into a box. It's time you use that supernatural strength to kick your way out."

A smile crept across her lips and she tilted her head. "What do you know about my supernatural strength, hmm?"

"You shoving me against a wall that night we met gave me a pretty good idea," he said with a smirk. "I was in equal parts aroused and terrified. A new combo for me."

Leona practically cackled at that. "Is that the way to your heart, Beliveau? Choking you up against a wall until you almost piss yourself with fear?"

"I did not almost *piss myself*," Sebastian hissed.

"Sure," she said, her eyebrows raised. "Whatever you say, darling."

His cheeks flushed, but he blamed it on the cold weather. "Your hands were freezing. Are you always so cold? You're wearing next to nothing."

"Yes, I'm always so cold. I'm a walking corpse, Sebastian. What do you expect?"

"The way your body works is simply astonishing," he said, looking her over. "I'd love to just see what's in there," he added, gesturing to her entire body. "Do you think it all looks the same? Your organs and stuff? Maybe it's all black or something…"

"*Now* who sounds like the murderer?"

"Mmm… still you."

Her smile broadened. "I've told you all about me but I hardly know anything about you."

"I can't spill *all* my secrets before the first date. I have to save something for the imagination."

"Come *on*," the redhead groaned. "Alright, tell me how you got so close to those blondes. Have you known them a very long time?"

Sebastian nodded and turned his attention back to the water as they continued walking. "Yeah. I've known Victor since I was eleven. I didn't have a normal or privileged upbringing. Or even middle class. Lower class might be a stretch, even," he muttered. "I stole a lot to get by, got mixed in with the wrong crowds. I went to one of the nicer neighborhoods one day, it was almost dark, and I was checking car doors to see if they were unlocked. Rich people don't tend to care about shit like that. I don't know why. Maybe because they can just replace whatever is stolen... or maybe they think their security measures are enough. Either way, I ended up, unknowingly, at Victor's house. He came out and caught me. Thank God it wasn't his dad or something."

"Was he angry?"

"No, actually..." Sebastian said, then he shook his head and laughed under his breath. "No, he's never really been angry with me. He just asked what I was doing."

"That's it?"

"Pretty much. He asked what I was doing, I told him I needed cash for food, and him not knowing any better, asked me why I didn't just eat the food I had at home," he laughed, glancing over at her. "Really showed both of us how the other half lives. Obviously, I told him we didn't have the luxury of a lot of food at home, and I never liked being at home anyway. Not when Dad was there at least. He told me I wouldn't find anything valuable in his parents' cars, but that I could come in for dinner. He told his mom I was a friend of a friend and that was that," he shrugged. "He is two years older than me. We've been inseparable ever since."

"That's nice," Leona said with a smile, reaching over to gently squeeze his arm. "Found family can often be better than blood family. I don't know what I would do without my girls."

"Yeah, I'm grateful for Victor and Charlotte both."

"Is Charlotte from here, too?"

"No, she's from New York. We all met in college up there. Instant connection."

"I can tell you're close. Did you and Charlotte ever…? Or Victor?"

"No, and no," Sebastian said. "You aren't the first person to think that. We're just all best friends. I've never had eyes for Charlie. I doubt she's ever thought of me that way either. Same for Victor. I could never betray either of them like that. No sex in the world is worth losing our bond for."

"Not many people share your loyalty," Leona complimented. "I'm glad you have them."

Sebastian resisted commenting on the irony, given *she* and her coven were about to take them away. He swallowed his resentment and gave into the pull he always felt around her. It almost felt even stronger now. "Those are all the secrets you get for the night, Abrin. I'll save the juicy stuff for our date."

Leona hummed in amusement and folded her arms. "So about this first date you keep mentioning…" she paused, arching her eyebrow. "I'm a very experienced woman. You can consider me wooed."

Sebastian scoffed. "You are most certainly *not* wooed. You're from the seventeenth century. You were probably courted and pined after by every man in the country."

"Well, maybe not *every* man…"

He rolled his eyes. "Whatever. My point is, while I'm flattered that you're so eager to throw me across a room into your coffin," he started, resisting a smirk at her glare, "that's not what's going to happen."

"What *is* going to happen then?"

Sebastian sighed and ran a hand through his hair. She never let him off the hook for anything. He moved his eyes to hers again and took a breath, his hands gently taking hers. "What's going to happen is I'm going to ask you out on a real date. And you are *hopefully* going to say yes. And then your crazy ex-boyfriend is going to try and murder me."

Leona was not *overly* amused at his last little quip, but the first part was so heartwarming that she overlooked it. "You aren't going to get down on one knee?"

"Would you like seeing me kneel before you, Leona?"

Leona would have blushed if she could. Shyly, she glanced away from him, before making eye contact again. "I would love nothing more than to go on a date with you, Sebastian Beliveau."

The man smiled and nodded his head. "Then prepare to be wooed, Leona Abrin."

11

Charlotte stood outside Sebastian's door and bounced on her heels in the chilly air. She looked around as she waited for him to answer the door, and spotted his elderly neighbor walking her dog down the sidewalk nearby. She lifted her hand in a wave and smiled. "Good morning, Mrs. Sodeko. How are you doing? How's Pookie?"

"Good!" the woman responded, waving in return. Her small Yorkie began yapping excitedly at the sight of a new person, and Charlotte gave an apologetic smile.

The door opened, causing her to whip her head back to the front. "Sebby, there you are. I was beginning to think you'd never answer the door. I was just checking up on you," she said, walking past him without an invite. She shed her coat and shivered, wrapping her arms around herself. "Jesus, Sebastian, how cold is it in here?"

"Sixty degrees," he said, then shut the door and locked it. He handed her her coat again. "You ought to get used to being cold. When you're a corpse, that's all you'll be."

"Don't start this with me," she said warningly, before sliding her arms back into her jacket. "Why do you have it so cold?"

"I'm trying to get used to the cold," he answered.

"Why? It's never cold in Louisiana. Except for, like, a month out of the year. Even then, it's chilly at best. Give or take a few days."

"*Because*—" he said pointedly, signaling her to stop making assumptions, "I intend to take Leona out on a date. And if we're going to be around each other, I'm going to need to get used to the cold. Have you touched one of them? They're freezing."

"Hold on," Charlotte said, a grin plastered across her pretty face. "You're just going to gloss over the fact that you're taking Leona on a *date*?!"

"It's not a big deal," he muttered, knowing she was going to react like this. It was part of the reason he'd been avoiding her, despite needing her help for the planning.

"It *absolutely* is a big deal, Sebby! What are you thinking of doing? What are you going to wear? If you're going to date her, are you going to let her turn you? How does this even work between a vampire and a human?"

"Take a breath," he said, putting his hands out to steady her shoulders. "Nobody's turning anybody. I do need your help with this though. I want you to be a part of it."

"I am *not* third-wheeling your first date in *forever*, Sebastian. No way."

"Not a third wheel," he reassured. "She was born hundreds

of years ago. At a time when balls and courting and all of these grandiose celebrations and gestures were a big thing. She never got to enjoy any of that, not really. I know how much you love to throw themed parties, so... I was thinking we could arrange an old English-style ball where we dress up. Skirts, corsets, powder, makeup... all of it. Do you think that's stupid?"

"Oh, Sebby," Charlotte said, placing her hand over her chest. If he didn't know better, he'd think she was about to cry. "I think that's beautiful. She's going to love it. When do you want to do it?

"Maybe this weekend... Saturday?"

"Perfect," she said, clasping her hands together. "I'll start getting invitations made. How many people do you want to show up?"

"You can invite whoever. But... the girls, obviously."

"Obviously," she teased. "We'll need to get you something to wear. Luckily, that won't be very hard to find in this city. You and Victor can go to the tailor together. I'll get a dress made and ordered for me. I'll also talk to the girls about what they want. I will help Leona find resources, but *you* will not be seeing the dress until the night of. It's bad luck otherwise."

"Charlie, we aren't getting married."

"Sebastian, you're about to hop in bed with a vampire. Marriage isn't *that* insane of a concept, all things considered."

He ignored that. They hadn't even kissed. They'd barely touched hands so far. Was this too much? Too fast?

"Thanks for your help, Charlie. I owe you," he finally said.

"You don't owe me anything, Sebby. You never have.

Seeing you happy is the only thanks I need," she said while smiling. "I really do want you to be happy. Whatever that means. You deserve it more than anyone I know."

"Thank you," he said softly. "You and Victor are everything to me. I don't know what I'd do without you."

"I know you're being sweet right now, but it also *sort of* feels like a guilt trip, so I'm going to ignore your last sappy statement," Charlotte teased, pinching his cheek gently. "Now then, enough of things that might make me cry. I will start on all of that and Victor will come back by to pick you up so you can get fitted. Okay?"

"Okay," he said. Sebastian watched her leave just as quickly as she came. He took a deep breath and closed his eyes, feeling overwhelmed with nerves all of a sudden. As much as he wanted to do this, he was extremely apprehensive. He had come off as cocky, but he was truly terrified that Gideon person would come for him. He supposed dying for a woman he liked wasn't that bad of a way to go, but he never thought he'd get caught up in the middle of a vampire love triangle.

Still, it was the most exciting his life had ever been.

He walked over to the sofa, sinking into the cushions. Picking up his phone from the simple, black coffee table, he checked for notifications. He had one from Leona, of course, who had just told him good morning. He enjoyed talking to her. They talked on the phone the last few nights after the river, and he'd found that he loved the sound of her voice. No matter how worried, anxious, or stressed he got, it all seemed to melt away the moment he heard her laugh on the other line. She had offered to come over, but he had insisted he wanted to do things the *right* way. As much as he'd love to bed her right in that moment, this was important to him. He knew, deep down, it was even more important to her. He wanted her to see that not all men were monsters. She was just as worthy of falling in love and being treated like a lady as anyone else was.

All of his life, Sebastian had wanted something similar. He wanted someone to share life with. Victor and Charlotte, of course, were major parts of his life, but they had each other. They were their own life partners. A perfect world to him would include his trio, plus the woman he chose to do life with. He couldn't help but wonder if Leona had come into his life for a reason. He had never believed in things like fate or destiny, but as he texted this vampire siren back, his beliefs began to expand.

Rather than tapping out a response to Leona's text, he clicked her contact info and started a phone call. It only rang once, before he heard her angelic voice on the other end greeting him.

"Didn't think you'd be awake just yet. It's barely daylight."

"Training," Sebastian said with a smirk. "I called Charlie over to talk to her about something. She goes on early-morning walks anyway, figured she could make a pit-stop."

"Everything okay?"

"More than okay," Sebastian reassured. He changed the subject so she stopped asking questions about what he and Charlotte met about. "What did you do all night then?"

Leona hesitated and briefly considered lying.

"It's okay if you ate. Or drank? What's the word?"

"We use 'fed' or 'feed,'" Leona responded. "But I did, in any case. You worked up my appetite along the river," she teased.

"How do you target people? How do the police not catch on?"

"Well, that's the good thing about this city... law enforcement is so corrupt, they don't give a shit. They see puncture wounds and assume it's drug-related. Bodies pop up around here all the time, and there's such a lack of police force that they don't care unless it's something huge. Bodes well for the girls and me because we can just follow any police or crime reports and pick and choose our victims from there."

"How do you find them from the reports?"

"It's not that difficult. We go to where the crime was reported and follow the scent from there. Longest it's ever taken me is about half a day, and that's just when multiple people are at a scene and I have to use the process of elimination to figure out who actually committed the crime."

"Why aren't you a detective?"

"I briefly considered it, among my extensive job history," Leona laughed. "I think it would draw too much attention. And if I found all the criminals and put them behind bars, where am I going to get my dinner?"

"Fair point," Sebastian conceded. "Do you ever feel guilty?"

"At first, yes," Leona said. "But... after a while, you get used to it. I can't get around it, and surviving off animal blood isn't sustainable. It's good in a pinch, but... there's nothing like human blood. It's the circle of life, I suppose."

Sebastian nodded, then walked through to his kitchen to start making his own breakfast. Cradling the phone between his cheek and shoulder, he opened the fridge. "Do you ever miss human food?"

"All the time. We didn't have nearly the options you lot have now. It's quite maddening to live in the worldwide hub for delicious food," she said with a light chuckle. "The smells aren't quite the same anymore. It's still good, but I don't get hungry and want blood or anything. I just appreciate it for what it is. We can eat, like I told you, but it's muted. I like gumbo."

"Really?" Sebastian laughed, raising his eyebrows. He nudged the fridge closed with his hip and set a carton of eggs down on the counter next to the stove. "A vampiress with a weakness for gumbo. What's next?"

"You don't even want to *know* my feelings on crawfish."

"In February we'll go on a food tour and find your favorites in the city," Sebastian promised. "Though, nothing is going to beat my gumbo recipe. Not that you'll appreciate it properly."

"I would love it if you cooked for me. And I'd appreciate every single second. Just like I do every other encounter with you."

"Alright, what do you want?"

"What?!"

"You're being *extra* flattery today. Spill. And it can't be my dick."

"You are such a man," Leona groaned. "I can't be nice to you without you thinking there's some ulterior motive? I'm crushed."

"Mhm," Sebastian hummed, the eggs sizzling on the pan as he cracked them in.

"Are you cooking now?"

"Yes. Just some eggs, I may throw some bread in the toaster. No blood though."

"I'd be concerned otherwise," Leona deadpanned. "Do you want me to let you go?"

"I feel like we both know letting each other go isn't exactly an option anymore. I know your big secret. And you know mine."

"Do I? Remind me."

"You forgot? Now *I'm* crushed."

"Sebastian!"

He smiled smugly to himself and crushed some of the egg yolks with his spatula to scramble them. "My secret is that I'm helpless to a pretty immortal who wants in my pants. Don't tell anyone though."

Leona giggled. "Your secret is safe with me."

Sebastian felt flush with happiness. "And you're safe with me."

12

*L*eona was practically on cloud nine.

She had spoken to Sebastian constantly since their night on the river and she felt like she was really getting somewhere with him. They were always asking each other questions, and the conversation flowed so naturally. He was the first person in a long time that genuinely made her laugh and smile. He *saw* her. She could still sense some apprehension from him when they were around each other, or when they video-called, but that was to be expected. She was just glad he wasn't running for the hills or reporting her to the authorities for murder or witchcraft.

They had been taking things somewhat slow, but that was more on Sebastian's end than hers. She had reassured him that just because she was born in another time, didn't mean he had to treat her that way. She was more than caught up to modern dating and how fast things tended to move these days. If he had wanted to ravish her right there on the riverbank, she wouldn't have had any protests. But he had insisted on 'doing things right' and Leona had been touched by that. Who was she to deny him of being a gentleman? Isn't that what she wanted all along?

Perhaps he was the one she'd been looking for.

She hoped so.

Leona looked up from the book she was poring over as a knock sounded from the front door. She closed the book and practically floated to the door, pulling it open. On the other side stood Sebastian, looking just as bewildered as he always did. Speak of the devil. A smile broke out across her lips and she tilted her head thoughtfully. "What a pleasant surprise, Beliveau."

Sebastian offered her a sloppy smile and a light blush. "I'm full of surprises, Abrin. But you can't tell anyone I'm here. I'm on strict confidential business," he said, his voice lowered.

"Oh?" Leona said, her eyebrows creeping up. She leaned forward just a bit and her voice dropped to a hushed tone. "What sort of confidential business?"

Sebastian reached into his inner coat pocket and pulled out an ornate piece of cardstock. He glanced down at it, before handing it to her.

Leona took it and looked down at it, her lips parting as she silently read the front.

Lover's Ball

The Company of Ms. Leona Abrin is Requested at Labasque
Manor, on Chartres Street, in the French Quarter, New Orleans, on
Saturday Evening, October 25th, 2014, at 7 o'clock

Victor Labasque
Charlotte Labasque

She looked up at Sebastian, her eyes misty. "This is a real invitation?"

"Yes," he said. "Piper and Whitney have theirs coming in the mail soon, but I wanted to hand-deliver yours. Charlotte made it *very* clear I was not to see you until the night of the ball, but I wanted to see your reaction. Is this too much?"

"Too much? Are you joking?" Leona said, her smile widening by the second. "This is just... lovely, Sebastian."

"Charlotte has been doing research to make it like the balls you were used to in your time as a human. I wanted to give you a sense of normality. And a memorable first date, considering I have hundreds — maybe thousands — of past first dates to compete with."

"Thousands is a bit insulting," Leona said. She suddenly threw her arms around his neck, causing Sebastian to tense up. It was such a stark reaction that she pulled back a little. "Sorry. Did I hurt you?"

"No," he said, his face unreadable. "It's fine," he murmured. Slowly, he snaked his arms around her waist to squeeze her back.

"Thank you," she whispered into his hair, staying in his arms. "You have no competition. I promise."

His smile was hidden in their embrace. A blanket of warmth washed over him, despite her frigid body temperature. He couldn't remember the last time somebody had hugged him. At least, not in a happy way. Usually any time Victor or Charlotte hugged him, it was because he was sad about something. The touch from Leona wasn't unwelcome, just unexpected.

But he could get used to it.

Slowly, she retreated from him and took a step back, her hands trailing down his arms. She smiled bashfully and clutched her invitation to her chest. An expectant look crossed her features as she watched him.

His daze from the hug faded and he cleared his throat. "I'd like to formally ask for your hand in this ball, Madame Abrin," he said, bowing his head.

Leona giggled and nudged his shoulder. "You are so cute. Nice try."

"I Googled it!" he laughed, lifting his head. "Is that not what they used to say?"

"More or less," she teased, before beaming at him. "I humbly offer my hand to you, Monsieur Beliveau. *Happily*."

Sebastian released a small breath and he gently took her hand. "See you Saturday evening, my lady," he purred, lowering his lips to the soft, pale skin of her knuckles.

She felt butterflies for the first time in three hundred years. Leona watched him walk down the pathway toward their front gate, then he disappeared down the street. She stood in the doorway for a while after that, her thoughts swimming in her head as a gentle breeze blew the leaves scattering the ground around her. She had been so apprehensive about returning to this place, about revisiting trauma that wasn't even Gideon-related by coming back. She had never been more grateful for something in all of her existence. Her eyes roamed around the trees looming over the middle of the street, bent by centuries of growth and history. The other houses lined the road, each looking different than the next. She always loved the personality New Orleans held, that every inch of it had its own story to tell. It reminded her so much of her childhood, of the life she missed so dearly; the life that was stolen from her.

But, for the first time in her immortal life, she was thankful she'd lived this long. She was hopeful for her future. Sebastian didn't treat her like she was damaged goods. He looked at her like he would any other normal woman. She was glad he didn't seem petrified with fear anymore. Just... mildly paralyzed in certain instances.

Her eyes cut down to the invitation in her hands. It was ornately designed with small imprints and lace around the sides. She could tell a calligrapher had decorated it by hand. It was truly one of a kind, and she was floored by how thoughtful Sebastian had been. He didn't have to go to so much effort, but he had. She had offered herself to him, no questions asked, and he'd refused under the guise of wanting to make an impression. She had never met a man as patient and kind as that, mortal or otherwise.

She knew that the moment she'd laid eyes on him, the reason she'd been so drawn to him at first sight, was because she fell in love.

Desperately, she wanted to believe he felt the same. Somewhere deep down.

"Tighter."

Leona gripped the poster on her bed, gritting her teeth as Piper pulled the strings of the corset vicing her body more taut. "It's not as if I have to breathe, is it? Tighter."

"If I pull it any tighter, you're going to implode," the blonde laughed. She tied up the back and pulled her to face her. She looked at her makeup and smiled happily. Her throat tightened with emotion and she gently pressed her hand to her cheek. "You look like yourself again. How I remember you when we first met."

"When we *first* met?" Leona said with an impish smirk.

Piper rolled her eyes. "Well... around that time. I suppose you were rather a bitch when we first met. And not at all in your skirts and bloomers and corsets."

"That man was mine and you know it."

"We have been over this. I saw him first. You just tried to swoop in and take my dinner."

"He was big enough for both of us."

"I still felt peckish afterward," she shrugged. "But of all the *beggars* who have tried to steal my food, you've been my favorite."

"Who's the bitch now?" Leona laughed. "But thank you for the compliment. I *feel* like myself again. I feel like the girl I used to be. Before the monster," she said, staring at herself in the mirror. "Do you think he'll like it?"

"Who, Sebastian? Please," Piper scoffed, standing behind her in the mirror. She squeezed the tops of her arms and rested her chin on her shoulder. "You might put him into cardiac arrest."

"Stop," she giggled. "Okay, let's get the dress on."

Piper opened up the wardrobe where the dress was hiding. It was a long-sleeved, black garment made entirely of silk and lace. It was cut off the shoulder with a low décolletage and a floor-length, bouffant skirt. The lace overlay was a deep emerald green, highlighting every asset of the dress. She had gotten it made special, and though it had cost a small fortune, it was worth it. If he had put in so much effort, she was going to return the favor. She was just glad she'd been able to get it done in time. As excited as she was about the date, half a week was *not* a lot of time to get a dress made in this style. Or any style, really.

"I'm so excited," Piper said with a grin, taking it out of the closet. "You look so authentic. Though *those* are quite modern," she said as she pointed to the black lingerie hanging on her hips. "Feeling hopeful?"

"Hush," Leona admonished. "They're nice. Aren't they nice?"

"Yes. I'm sure Sebastian will think so too."

"I doubt he'll see them," she said, carefully stepping into the dress as Piper helped hoist it up her body.

"Why?" she asked, fastening all the ties on the back.

"He just doesn't seem interested. In *that* way, at least. I mean, he *does*, and I love that he's being so polite, but... I would expect a delay like this from someone from *our* time, but his? We've been talking nonstop for weeks now. The most we've done is hold hands. I have half-wondered if he's gay."

Piper burst out laughing, even when Leona swore at her to be respectful. "Sweetheart, he threw an entire ball in your honor. If that's not a horny man, I don't know what is. Do you really think he'd go through all this trouble just to be your *friend*?"

"He said he wants to woo me, but… I don't know," she sighed. "Maybe I'm just being silly about all this. What would he want with me? And everything that comes with me?"

"Pfft," Piper scoffed. "*Please.* You don't give yourself enough credit. Sebastian knows what he signed up for, and he's still bending over backward for you. You're always going on about how you want a man who's both soft but bold enough to protect you. If you want him that bad, why don't you just glamour him a little?"

"Piper!"

"Not a crazy amount! Just… enough to give him a little nudge. He might need that. You *are* pretty intimidating."

"Absolutely not. And don't you do anything to him either. I want him to come to me of his own accord."

"Such a hopeless romantic," the other woman said, shaking her head. "You're ready to go."

Leona smoothed her hands over the front of the dress. Her hair was curled and styled up, with beaded jewelry glittering throughout to give her an extra pop. She had an emerald pendant shimmering against her chest, completing the look.

"When is Whitney supposed to be back?" Leona asked, moving to help Piper into her dress. She was wearing a similarly designed dress, but it was white with floral accents. Her blonde hair was curled and down for the occasion.

"She called and said she would be back in time for the ball. She might be bringing Damien. She said they were fighting, but you know how that goes," Piper said while rolling her eyes.

"Let's hope she leaves him in whatever hovel he's undoubtedly staying in at the moment," Leona muttered.

It put her on edge, the thought of Damien being near her. Though she wasn't his biggest fan, he wasn't as bad as Gideon. He meant well — most of the time — and didn't enjoy pure torture like his best friend did. Her reservations with him came mostly from how badly he treated Whitney and the fact that she couldn't stay away from him.

The fact that he was a werewolf was beside the point.

"She's going to reek of dog," Piper grimaced, shaking her head. "I could never."

"The heart wants what the heart wants," Leona shrugged.

"You'd know," Piper said with a smile. She walked over to the mirror and checked out her reflection. "This thing hides my ass."

"It hides a lot of things," Leona said with a light laugh. "I think your face does enough talking for the rest of your body anyway."

Piper gave her a look and fluffed her hair, before turning to face her. "Ready to—"

Ding!

Leona glanced toward the window that faced the front porch. "Who's that? Are you expecting someone?"

"No. Not anyone that would ring the doorbell," Piper said, picking up her dress so she could walk to the window. She peered down and a small smile spread across her lips. "Oh. It's for you."

"For me?" Leona asked, her heart dropping into her stomach.

"Don't panic," Piper said, her head whipping to her best friend at the tone of her voice. "Just go down and see. I'd never send you into danger. But it looks like it's supposed to be a surprise."

Leona trusted her implicitly. She walked through the bedroom door, carefully maneuvering the stairs in her heels and skirt. She flung the door open and gasped, her eyes wide with delight as she took in the scene before her.

Sebastian was there, dressed in a fine black suit, complete with emerald accents to match her dress. A green cravat tie was fastened around his neck, the stitching on his coat was black, and his dress shoes were dark, but shimmered green *just* enough when the light hit them right. His hair was curled and styled, sitting just at his shoulders.

Behind him on the street was a horse-drawn carriage and driver awaiting them. Sebastian smiled at her and held out a bouquet of red roses. "Your chariot awaits, my lady."

"Sebastian!" Leona squealed, rushing down the steps of the porch. She practically jumped into his arms, unable to show her gratitude and excitement in any other way.

The man laughed softly and wrapped his free arm around

her waist, trying to be mindful of both the flowers and her outfit. He had nearly lost his footing and assumed she had pulled her strong hug back at the last possible second. It still had been like getting tackled by a linebacker. "I take it you like the surprise?"

"Yes," she breathed, inhaling the scent of him. She could *smell* sunlight and life on him. It was mixed with an earthy cologne, one that reminded her of sandalwood and vanilla. She pulled back just a bit, staying in his strong embrace. Peering into those dark brown eyes of his, she, for once, felt like she lost the ability to breathe. To think. Her eyes slowly trailed down his face to his lips, then back up to his eyes. She could count the little hairs speckled around his eyebrows, a few sparsed in the middle. He was clean-shaven, his cheeks peppered with small, dark remnants of facial hair. His hair was styled and she could smell the product spread throughout his black locks.

He was just… radiant.

"Hey! Good job, Sebby!" Piper called from the doorway, before wolf-whistling.

Their spell was broken and Sebastian released Leona. He handed her the flowers and looked behind her toward her blonde partner in crime. "Don't call me that."

"Why not?" Piper asked, coming down the steps. "Charlotte calls you that."

"Exactly. Other people do not."

"Not even Leona? I call her Le. There's nothing wrong with it."

Sebastian shook his head. "No. Leona's name is so

beautiful, every syllable deserves its own spotlight. To shorten it would be a crime," he said.

Leona could have cried. She leaned into him and glanced at Piper. "Listen to what he says, Pipe. Sebastian wants to be called Sebastian."

"How about 'asshole?'" Piper muttered. "Alright, let's get going. We don't want to be late."

"This carriage isn't for you," Sebastian said gruffly. "You'll need to find your own ride."

"Seriously?" Piper said, looking to Leona for help. The redhead merely shot her an apologetic glance, but she agreed with Sebastian. She wanted to share in this moment alone with him. This was *their* night. Piper would get over it.

"Dickhead might be a better name," the blonde said, cutting her eyes away from them. "*Fine*. Enjoy your journey, lovebirds. I'll see you two at the manor," she said. In a moment, she was gone. Thankfully, the carriage driver wasn't paying attention.

"Sorry about her," Leona sighed, cradling the flowers.

"It's alright. Not the first time I've pissed a woman off."

"Is that so?"

Sebastian's lips quirked slightly in amusement. "No. I lied," he said. "Unless you count Charlotte. I *live* to annoy her."

"Now *that* I believe," she laughed. "Let me put these in a vase and then we can go."

Sebastian sprung into action and he took her hand, helping her back up the porch steps. If he was going to do this, he was going to go *all out*. He walked in with her and fetched the vase she directed him to. Filling it with water, he carefully placed the flowers inside. "Perfect," he said to himself, arranging them in the middle of her dining table. "Is this a good space?"

"Perfect," she repeated with a smile. She held out her hand to him. "Shall we then, my lord?"

Sebastian flushed. "We shall, my lady," he said, taking her hand so he could lead her back out to the carriage.

They ventured outside into the crisp, autumn air and he helped her step up into the carriage. He climbed in on the other side and they were off. The clopping of the horses' hooves echoed around the quiet streets. It was a bit early for the French Quarter to come alive, so things were peaceful. They wouldn't stay that way, of course, especially on a weekend so close to Halloween, but he relished in the tranquility they were offered in the moment.

"Thank you."

Sebastian looked over at Leona. He smiled slightly and nodded. "Of course. I want you to be happy. You deserve it."

"I mean it, Sebastian. Nobody has ever gone to this much effort for me. Not even Gideon, before…"

"I'm not Gideon," he said, shifting so he could face her a little more. "And I never will be."

"Thank God for that," she sighed in relief. Her head turned to look at the passing scenery, the people walking by and gawking at them, the trees, the faint music playing from a mystery corner. "I love this city. It's the only place that has a soundtrack no matter where you go."

That amused him. "I never thought about it that way,

but you're right. There's always some jazz band playing somewhere in earshot."

She smiled wistfully, a few ringlets swaying in the wind. "I would love nothing more than to just finish my days out here. Not having to look over my shoulder. Just... normal. That's all I've ever wanted."

Sebastian watched her closely, his eyes scanning over her features. He didn't have anything to say in response, so he merely listened. He wished he could see what she had been like in her true youth. Would she have given him a passing glance? He had gathered that vampires were made perfect, and all their human imperfections were washed away with the transformation. He couldn't imagine any part of her being classed as a blemish. She had a defined jawline, her lips were a perfect, pale pink cupid's bow, and her eyes were the most beautiful green crystals he'd ever seen. She was completely mesmerizing. He appreciated that her vampiric traits hadn't destroyed some of the finer parts of her countenance: the freckles dotting her cheeks, her eyelashes long enough to create hurricanes, her dark, auburn eyebrows that arched perfectly, framing her eyes in a way unlike any other.

"We've arrived."

His daydream ended and he focused on their surroundings, seeing the Labasque Manor lit up and decorated for the occasion. He'd never tire of seeing this home. The lanterns adorning the columns in the entryway were alight and flickering. He could hear the dull roar of music from the inside, and there were even people milling around the front yard, sharing in cigarettes, laughter, drinks, or all three.

"Thank you," he said to the driver, slipping him some cash for a tip. He hopped down from the carriage and hurried to the other side. Gripping her tightly, he helped her down to the ground, making sure she was steady. Their arms looped together and they approached the doorway.

As they entered, they were met with bright lights, servants wandering around carrying trays of drinks and food, and many people donning Victorian-style ballgowns and suits. Everything looked *perfect*. He hoped she thought so too.

"Oh my goodness," Leona whispered in awe, her eyes wide with wonder as she looked around.

Sebastian's chest swelled with pride as he looked at her, and he had never seen something more beautiful.

At that moment, he realized he was falling in love with her.

13

"Hey, you made it!" Charlotte squealed in delight as she found Sebastian and Leona at the entrance, taking it all in. She took Leona's hands in hers and grinned. "Well? What do you think?!"

"It's breathtaking," Leona said honestly, looking at her. "Thank you so much."

"You really outdid yourself, Charlie," Sebastian agreed. He needn't voice his thanks, he knew she already knew how grateful he was.

Everything was going off without a hitch. People were bustling around, enjoying living in another time period. He hoped it didn't dredge up any bad memories for Leona and make her sad. That's the last thing he wanted.

"Would you care to dance?" Sebastian asked, holding his hand out to Leona. "I have already told Charlotte *not* to make a big announcement in your honor."

"He made me promise," the blonde huffed.

Leona smiled and took his hand. "Thank you. I would love to dance."

They walked out to the middle of the ballroom and fell into step together. Leona gently placed a hand on Sebastian's shoulder as her other one gripped his tightly. His hand settled on her waist and the other kept her hand company. They stepped in time together, flowing perfectly with those waltzing around them.

"I want to know more about you," Sebastian said as he looked down at her.

"What do you want to know? You know I'm an open book for you, Seb."

His head quirked a bit and the corners of his mouth upturned slightly. "Seb?"

"Oh no. Is that one of your off-limits nicknames?"

"No," he laughed. "Nobody has ever called me that. Charlie calls me Sebby and Victor goes for Bas sometimes. Never Seb."

"Can I call you Seb?"

"Sure. That'll be off-limits for you."

"I'll take it."

She smiled widely at him, her lipstick still perfectly in place. "Why does Charlotte call you Sebby?"

"God knows," he said, shaking his head. "Vic and I met her in college in New York a decade ago. She kept calling me 'adorable,' and it always pissed me off. So she coupled that with 'Sebby' and it just stuck. I don't mind it so much now. But she's the only one I'll allow to get away with it."

"You *do* look like a Sebby."

Sebastian glared at her, but the expression melted with her giggles. He pulled her closer to him and they spun around once. "You changed the subject. Tell me more about you. I know I ask questions about your *present*, but what about your past? What was your family like?"

"For the record, *you* changed the subject," Leona teased, earning her an unamused look. "My family was fairly normal. I had a sister called Petrie. My father was Robert and my mother was Daisy. We weren't peasants, but we weren't any sort of royalty. We got by just fine, had a small-sized estate. We did have this large garden in the back where I spent much of my time as a girl. The flowers were just beautiful. My mother really lived up to her namesake," she said fondly. "We never wanted for anything material, but we also never asked for things outside our reach. I took it for granted. I always dreamed of something outside of my mundane life. I wanted to travel, I wanted to marry a rich lord, and ride horses all over the world. I wanted adventure."

She sighed sadly to herself, thinking about it. "But of course, when I met Gideon, everything changed. He was my sense of adventure. I was a fool."

"You didn't know," he said reassuringly.

"Still," she shrugged. "I miss them dearly. When Gideon changed me, he planted some story that I had a riding accident and was too mangled to be seen. My parents and sister mourned me deeply. It was horrific to watch from a distance. He forbade me from seeing them after I turned. He said it went against our laws. I later found out that no such laws existed — outside of his personal reign. I watched them for years after that. I was there when my father died, my mother, and eventually, my sister. Gideon disappeared from their life soon after I 'died.' I always wonder what they thought. If they truly believed that I was dead or if they were suspicious… But I'll never know."

Sebastian regarded her thoughtfully. It broke his heart. He couldn't imagine sitting on the sidelines, waiting for his loved ones to die. Not getting to say goodbye. He didn't have the same poetic relationship with his blood family, but he would absolutely feel the same way about losing Charlotte and Victor.

"What about your family?" Leona asked, sliding her hand from his shoulder to the back of his neck. Her fingers toyed with the curls she found.

"Charlotte and Victor are all I have. My parents are long dead," he admitted. "My father was an abusive alcoholic the world is better off without. My mother was a frail, scared woman who was too weak to protect her son and stand up to her own husband. They got married out of principle. I wasn't planned, so he wanted to make an honest woman out of her. I wish he hadn't," he sighed. "I didn't spend much time at home from the time I was a teenager to when I went to college. Victor's family practically adopted me. He taught me manners, how to conduct yourself in public, and that even if you didn't have money, you could still trick people into *thinking* you had money. So I sat up straight, I came out of my shell and learned how to negotiate a deal, I learned how to schmooze politicians. All of it."

"But… you work with art," Leona said.

"I do," he said. "But it wasn't always that way. I wanted to be like Victor. I wanted to be successful. I didn't want to *act* like I had money, I wanted to *have* money. I wanted to have everything I'd ever wanted. When I was younger, I thought money was the key to everything: a happy life, success, love. I found out it wasn't. I pursued my passions, and Victor and Charlotte both encouraged that. He has never tried to make me into something I'm not. I cannot say the same for the other people that have flitted in and out of my life."

Leona carefully played with the locks between her slim fingers. "How did your parents die?"

Sebastian sighed. He hadn't ever told this story before. The only two people who really knew everything *experienced* it happening. He wasn't sure where to begin.

"It happened after I got home from college. My dad came home too drunk, stumbling in in the middle of the night. The only reason I was even at the house was because Victor and Charlotte were celebrating graduation with his parents and I didn't want to intrude. My mother requested me home so she could do something similar for me, though we just shared in a cheap bottle of wine and talked. It was always easier when it was just us at home. She was more relaxed. I tried to protect her, but after a while… it just became impossible. A growing boy should not have to worry about fending off a grown man from beating him and his mother to a pulp," he muttered. "But… he came home and they got into a fight. I was about to leave when things just… shifted. It was worse than it had ever been before. He was accusing her of all sorts: cheating, stealing his money, abuse. I didn't believe a word of what I heard... but even if it had been true, nobody deserved that betrayal more. Things escalated and escalated until I heard this loud pop. Then two more. I ran into the room and saw my mother on the floor in a pool of her own blood. Shot dead. The bullets killed her instantly. My dad turned the gun on me and I tackled him to the ground. I just... saw red," he said, his eyes distant. As if he were back in that moment again. "I got the gun from him after it went off a few times. I still don't know how it didn't get me. All I remember is pulling the trigger as many times as I could toward him and... that was it," he said. "Both of them... gone in an instant."

Leona stared at him, completely horrified. How could a man so sweet and gentle have such a turbulent youth? How had he come out so... normal?

"The police came and arrested me. I have a record so it was expected. I called Victor in a panic when I got booked into the jail, and he bailed me out. He paid off the courts and the district attorney and made everything go away. The justice system is so corrupt in the parish that I'm not sure if a jury could have been convinced of self-defense."

"How could you possibly get off on a murder charge? It *was* self-defense, but..."

"The unknown power of a family in all the high places," Sebastian teased, but the smile didn't quite reach his eyes. "Victor has never gone into much detail about how he pulled it off. But I know that money talks, and the Labasques have more money than I can even comprehend. I had to do some community service, but that's a far cry from life in prison.

From the small parts Vic's told me, his dad went and sweet-talked the DA. They're pretty good friends, given his father is also a politician, but... I shudder to think about how many zeros were on the check he had to have written."

"Wow," Leona said. "Well... I'm glad you're not in prison."

Sebastian chuckled softly. "That makes two of us. After all of that got brushed under the rug, I officially moved into the Labasque Manor and tried to regain my footing. They helped me build my art business and soon I got enough money to move out. They offered to buy me a home, furnish it, everything, but I wanted to do it off my own back. I owe them everything I have," he said. "You can understand why I am not giving up their mortality so easily."

Leona frowned and moved both her hands to cradle his cheeks. "Thank you for telling me, Sebastian. I know that couldn't have been easy to relive. I feel much closer to you now," she murmured. "You are a wonderful man. Though we've only known each other for a few weeks, I feel like I've known you my whole life. There's nothing you could say that could scare me away."

Sebastian leaned into her touch, his entire body melting. She was like a warm blanket on a snowy day. Everything around him ceased to exist when he looked into those gorgeous, bright eyes. He gently moved his hand to hold the back of her head, the other one sliding around her waist to pull her closer. Dipping his head down, he leaned closer to her, Leona's eyes fluttering closed as she gave into his touch. The distance between them almost closed—

"Well, well, what *is* going on here?"

Sebastian didn't recognize the voice, but when Leona immediately tensed, as if fear had completely paralyzed her, he knew who this was.

Gideon.

ebastian stared at the beast of a man. He was taller than him by several inches, his hair dark and cut around his slightly pointed ears. His eyes were as dark as blood, peering into his soul as if he owned his entire being. He was wearing a suit of the deepest purple, so much so that it looked black in the right lighting. Sebastian could just tell this *creature* was dangerous. He felt stricken with fear, but compelled to hold eye contact. He assumed Gideon was taking advantage of his powers against him.

"Don't be rude, my Leona flower. Aren't you going to introduce me to your new... *toy*?"

Leona instinctively moved closer to Sebastian, standing slightly in front of him. "What the hell are you doing here?" she hissed.

"Well, Whitney had to come back for a party and Damien was *so* upset at her early departure. I wanted to see what sort of event was *so* important that it tugged her away from her mate. Dame has been pouting for the last six hours. He'll be pleased to know that this was well worth the escape," Gideon said smugly, his eyes moving to scan over the room. "Is this where you live now?"

"No," Leona said. She didn't want him anywhere near this home, these people. Sebastian. "You need to leave, Gideon. *Right now.*"

The man smirked and finally turned his attention to Sebastian. "Gideon Valdis."

"I know who you are," Sebastian ground out, his hand laced tightly with Leona's. "And you were not invited."

Gideon full-on *bellowed* at him, his hand moving over his chest. His pale fingers were topped with long, pointed nails. He was a vampire in every sense of the word. "Leona, sweetheart, this is so adorable. A human bodyguard. A bit of an oxymoron, but I'll play along," he said, then shifted his attention to Sebastian. He stepped close to him and in a flash, brought his hand up *millimeters* from his face.

Sebastian did not flinch.

Gideon raised an eyebrow and scoffed, before grabbing him. He nearly hoisted him up off the ground, Sebastian's tiptoes brushing against the floor. "Still want to protect her now, human?"

"With my dying breath," Sebastian ground out, glaring at him all the same. "I told you to leave. It would be in your best interest to do as I say."

The tall vampire focused on Sebastian, holding his gaze as he regarded him carefully. Hungrily. Sebastian saw something flash in those red eyes of his. He almost wanted to say it was recognition, but that wouldn't make any sense. Surely if Gideon already knew who he was, he wouldn't be putting on a show like this, and he wouldn't be allowing him to live any longer. Honestly, Sebastian was rather confused as to why he was letting him live at all. Though, Leona had said he liked to play with his food. Now he understood.

Gideon lowered him and grinned. "Leona, where *do* you find these men? This is the first one that actually has some nerve, I'll give him that. Or perhaps he's too stupid to understand what's going on."

"Gideon," Piper said from behind him. "Leave Sebastian and Leona alone. If you came here to cause trouble, then you need to go. Nobody has bothered you. You're the one who showed up unannounced," she said firmly.

Gideon turned his head to look at her, then slowly released Sebastian. "Fine, fine... I was just having a little fun," he laughed, putting his hands up. "Nobody can take a joke around here anymore. But if Leona wants to play with her food a little longer, that's fine. I'm a patient man," he said, eyeing Leona intensely. "You and I are going to need to have a talk though. It seems you've forgotten our *understanding* with each other. You should know better than to try and hide."

Sebastian stood in front of Leona and squared up to him. "You don't speak for her anymore. Say something else, I *beg* you."

"You really are stupid, aren't you?" Gideon cooed.

"Let's find out," he said, holding eye contact. "I will not ask you to leave again."

"I could kill you here and now, boy. You wouldn't even

know what happened."

"Here I stand. Give it your best shot."

Gideon let out an amused breath and he looked over Sebastian's shoulder to Leona. "I think I like him. Good choice." He nudged Sebastian back with one finger, the strength causing the mortal man to stumble back into Leona. The woman steadied him and held him close against her chest.

"Enjoy your meal, flower," Gideon said, his gaze locked on Leona like a lion stalking its prey. "I'll come back for you later."

In a moment, the space where he stood was empty. Whitney stood, horrified, from beside Piper. She hadn't given any sort of information away to Damien, merely told him she had to go. He had accused her of cheating, to which she merely scoffed at and left. She should have known better than to think he would let it go. Why had she been so *stupid*? She had garnered Gideon's attention through her idiotic boyfriend's tantrum and now... now she was potentially the reason Leona got dragged back to England and Sebastian ended up a bloodied puddle on the floor.

"Clear the party," Piper said. Charlotte, Victor, and Whitney were nearby, having watched the entire encounter unfold. "We need to talk *now*."

"Turn us!" Victor said as they gathered in the kitchen of the manor. "There's no time to waste. That prick is back and knows where we are. You need help. An army."

"Nobody's making an army," Leona said, her head resting against her hand. She yearned for something as simple as a migraine at that moment. "Gideon is *my* problem. I knew I should have never come here."

"Stop it," Sebastian said. "Gideon is *all* of our problems now. You came here and that's how it is. We need to figure out how to either hide you or fight him."

"Perhaps Victor has a point, Leona," Piper said. Whitney had been quiet thus far, the guilt of being what led Gideon to their gates eating her alive. "You and I both know that Gideon will stop at nothing until he has you under his thumb again. Sebastian might have squeaked by tonight sheerly by *amusing* him, but that will get old quickly. He needs protection, or else he's going to suffer a fate far worse than death."

"No," Sebastian said whilst standing up. "I'm not going to be the reason you murder my friends."

"It's not up to you, Seb—" Charlotte started, but stopped when Sebastian lost his temper.

"NO!" he boomed, silencing the room. He seemed to gather himself and he took a deep breath, his chest heaving slightly. "No," he said in a quieter voice. "I will not be the reason you die."

"I can't do this again. I don't want to be here. I don't want to talk about this," Leona said, growing upset. The thought of losing Sebastian to something other than natural causes *decades* from now was too much to bear. She knew better than to run from Gideon. He would kill Sebastian purely to spite her and torture her, no matter if she ran into his arms freely at this very moment. It was too late for apologies. She would rather endure a hundred centuries in Gideon's castle than sign Sebastian's death warrant.

However, it looked like she already had.

"He has to have a weakness," Sebastian said. "He has to."

"He doesn't," Whitney said from the corner of the room. "There's a reason he's been alive for millennia. Nobody has stood a chance. Damien is the only one who has ever come close. And…"

"And what?" Sebastian asked.

Whitney regarded him thoughtfully. "Nothing. I'm trying to say it's pointless."

"I don't buy that," he snapped. "At all. This is insanity," he said. His heart had been racing at a dangerous level ever since that monster had snuck into their doors. He was scared. "How do you kill one of your kind? A normal vampire."

"Fire is the most effective option. Destroying beyond recognition or reincarnation. From the few times I've done it, I've ripped the extremities off and burned everything I could until it was nothing but ash. It's similar if we stay out in the sun for too long," Whitney responded.

"Okay, so why don't you just go rip him apart and throw him in a giant fire?" Sebastian asked whilst throwing his hands up.

"That's easier said than done," Piper scoffed. "You think it's easy to kill a vampire? Especially him? We can't just go up to him and rip an arm or two off. He has to be incapacitated first for us to even come close. Nobody's gotten that far. Obviously."

"I want to go home," Leona said quietly. Sebastian came

back to earth and looked at Leona. He'd never seen her this way before. She seemed so *small*.

"He doesn't know where I live. Come with me," Sebastian said.

Piper looked uneasy at that suggestion. "Regardless of her location, he can find her if he really wants to. Leona, you need to at least come with us so you can have some sort of protection. Perhaps we can call Damien and Theodore... see if they can distract him for a few more years. Enough for us to develop a plan."

"All hell is going to break loose," Whitney said with a frown. "The whole reason we're in this situation is because of Damien anyway. He will not fight with us or against us. He will disappear like he always does when we need him most. Then he'll turn up when the dust has settled. And Theo won't fight Damien, so..."

"She's coming home with me," Sebastian said. "You can discuss your method of attack without us."

Grabbing Leona's hand, he led her out of the room and into the street. He would not let harm befall her.

15

Leona walked into Sebastian's house silently, her movements rigid and tense. She looked down at her big dress and felt like it was poisoned. She didn't want anything on her that had been in the same room as *him*. Her eyes followed Sebastian as he locked the door, then went to check around the house to make sure they were alone.

She hurriedly yanked the sleeves down her arms. It was like she was being burned worse than the sun. Reaching behind her, she fingered the knots of the ties in the back, loosening them until the dress pooled at her feet. She did the same with the corset, her body relaxing. She stepped out of the offending garments, clad only in her black lace panties. She started to take those off too when Sebastian came back in and abruptly stopped in his tracks.

"Oh," he said dumbly, before quickly turning to protect her modesty. "Sorry, I didn't know you were… disrobing," he mumbled.

For the first time since Gideon showed up, she let a soft smile grace her lips. She was so protective of this man. She wouldn't allow anything to happen to him. "I'm not used to covering up. Men don't usually complain," she teased, bending down to pick up her clothes.

"That wasn't a complaint," he said, still turned away from her. "Do you want to wear something of mine? I'm afraid I can't concentrate with you naked in my living room."

Leona bunched her clothes up in front of her and nodded. "Yes, Sebastian. That would be nice. Thank you."

He led her to his bedroom and fetched a pair of his boxers and a simple, black t-shirt. He cut his eyes away from her as she dropped her clothes and took the items from him. She rivaled Charlotte as far as confidence went. He couldn't count the number of times he'd seen the blonde just wandering nude around her house. It was her right, of course, and he'd have never done anything untoward against her, but it didn't stop him from feeling uncomfortable. Victor had never seen him as a threat, and he was confident in their marriage, so he never batted an eye. Sebastian had also walked in on them more times than he could even remember, much to his chagrin. Some of those instances were seared into his brain forevermore.

When Leona was dressed, she began folding up her dress. It was a shame it was tainted now, it was beautiful and expensive. "I'm decent now, Seb," she said. "Thank you for being such a gentleman," she added as he turned back around. "And thank you for being so brave back there. I'm sorry he hurt you. It is extremely difficult for me to retaliate against him. Fledglings are compelled to protect their sires. It goes against my genetic code to fight him."

"You call him 'sire?'" Sebastian asked, helping her fold.

"I try not to," Leona said, sporting a laugh laced with zero humor. "He doesn't deserve such an honor. But technically, yes, he is my sire. I am his fledgling. That's what the creators, createes call themselves. Since he made me, my instincts try to prevent me from harming him. He's too powerful for me anyway," she said sadly. "I have never stood a chance. He just finds my protests amusing. It's another chance for him to show off his power."

"I could feel some sort of pull against me when I looked at him. Almost like he was willing me to bend to him. Is that part of your power?"

"Yes," Leona said, sinking down onto the edge of his bed. "It's part of our predatory capabilities. We lure you to do what we wish, then we strike. It makes the hunt a little easier. I'm sure he was willing you to step aside, hence his anger when you didn't. I'm surprised those powers didn't work on you. They certainly work on everyone else, immortals included."

"Maybe I'm just special," Sebastian teased, trying to lighten the mood. He sat down next to her and angled his body toward her, their knees touching. "I wasn't about to sit back and let him take you again. I promised you that he wouldn't harm you ever again. I meant that."

"You said you'd protect me with your dying breath. Did you mean that?"

He looked into her eyes and nodded. "Every word."

Leona shuddered out a long breath, before slipping her

hands into his. She squeezed them gently. "I want to show you something, Sebastian. I can't... do this with you until I do. You should know everything about me."

"Nothing is going to scare me away, Leona," he reassured.

"Just let me show you." She reached up and placed her hands on either side of his face. Pressing her thumbs into his cheeks, she focused hard on his eyes. Sebastian's pupils dilated, and then his eyes glazed over. She could tell by his expression that he was in her head, seeing everything she'd been through.

1704.

"Come with me, darling. I want to show you something," Gideon said to a much more vibrant Leona. Her red hair had a sheen to it that gave off life. Her cheeks were rosy and the smile on her face actually reached her eyes.

"What are you showing me, my love?" Leona beamed, hanging off his arm like he was the greatest thing in the world. To her, he was. "More flower arrangements? I believe we'll have every gardener in the country working our wedding!"

"In here," Gideon said, ignoring her comments and leading her to a darkened room in the basement of his estate. It was lined with barrels of wine, racks of bottles of various alcohol. The floors were pebbled with cobblestones of varying colors and textures. He let Leona go in before him, then he shut and locked the door behind him. No sunlight came into the room. No moisture. The only light sources were sconces lit in every corner.

"What is this place, Gideon?" Leona asked, looking around. "Wine cellar? I've never been in here before."

"In a sense," he said. "You know I want to be with you forever."

"Of course," she said, turning to face him with a smile. "The wedding is in a week. Are you getting cold feet?"

"Not at all," he replied. Slowly, he took her hand, relishing the warmth of her skin. He could feel the life pulsing through her. "I really do mean forever."

"So do I."

He pulled her close against him, dipping his head down so he could kiss her neck. Leona giggled and squirmed, playfully attempting to nudge him away. It was improper for a lady to accept such forward advances from the man she courted, especially so close to their wedding day. Gideon had stolen a few kisses and touches over the last four years, but overall, he had behaved like a perfect gentleman. She was head over heels in love.

His kisses got a bit more insistent and hard. Leona's giggles faded and she worked a little harder to push him off. "Gideon, you're hurting me," she said, her voice wavering with a lilt of fear. "Gideon. Stop," she said firmer. His grip was like iron melded around her body. She cried out as she felt a searing pain in her neck, as if she'd been stabbed. "Gideon!" she protested, thrashing as much as she could in his vice. The man didn't let go, and eventually, the room began to spin. Black spots flecked her vision and she felt her legs go weak. Collapsing against him, her eyes fluttered, her skin pale. "Gideon," she whispered.

"Shhh," he soothed, pulling back from her, his chin glistening with blood. "I'll be here when you wake up."

Sebastian jolted slightly in his trance, tears streaming down his cheeks. His body tensed and began to tremble in pain. His breathing hitched, then got heavy and rapid. His eyes were moving back and forth and paralysis took over

It was the worst pain he'd ever felt in his life. It was mixed with terror, betrayal, and regret. Through his veins, he could feel an insidious presence creeping its way in. A hundred spiders filled with venom invaded his body, biting every inch they could. His heart stopped and constricted in a way that made breathing a thing of the past. His body felt both ablaze with white fire, but frozen inside the sharpest glaciers. He made a small noise in discomfort, only because the scream begging to be let out died on his tongue. The tears were flowing rapidly now, dripping down onto his thighs.

Leona opened her eyes as an immortal, and the first thing she saw was darkness.

She was alone.

Pushing herself to sit up, she looked around. The sconces were dimmed to embers now. Her eyes adjusted to the darkness instantaneously, and she could see every fleck of dust in the air; every grain of dirt wedged between the grout of the flooring; every knot in the wooden barrels containing something she knew not to be wine. Her eyes moved to the bottles lining the racks in the room, the red, deep glint of their contents suggesting something other than wine as well.

She inhaled, though no breath entered her lungs. Only scents. The deep, earthy wisps of dirt, trees, the remnants of sunlight. She could smell her own blood, and the blood hidden in the room.

Though the room was barren of windows, she knew it was nighttime. Closing her eyes, she listened, giving in to these new senses. She heard the hum of insects outside, the rustling of leaves in the trees that lined Gideon's estate, the creaking of the upper half of the castle.

Her hands felt along the rough stone flooring, the dirt particles rubbing against every fiber of her skin. Suddenly, she brought her hands up to her neck, but there was no wound there. Her fingers traced her skin, which was colder than she'd ever felt before. Everything was pristine, smooth, unblemished. If she wasn't inundated with a plethora of new, heightened senses, she would have thought she just woke up from a nightmare.

"Gideon?" she whispered, only to be met with silence.

The room felt hollow. She pushed herself to stand, feeling both weaker and stronger than she ever had before all at the same time. She maneuvered through the room to the door, pulling at the handle. It was locked. Claustrophobia set in and she frantically looked around, searching for any way out. Where was Gideon? What had he done to her? Why had he done this?

With her panic increasing, Leona gripped the door again and pulled as hard as she could. The hinges exploded and the wood splintered, causing the door to fly past her and out of her grip. It crashed into the liquids being kept across the room and broke them open. Suddenly, she was so overwhelmed with hunger and thirst that it froze her in place. Her pupils dilated almost completely, her green irises a mere halo around the eclipse that had found its way *into her eyes. Instead of leaving, she turned on her heel, back to the place she'd been on the floor. In a flash of movement, she was on her hands and knees, licking up the blood pooling on the ground. A frenzy overtook her body, her senses, her soul, and she lapped up everything she could like a woman starved.*

"Christ, Leona," a voice said in disgust from the doorway. She whipped her head around, her face and body covered in blood now. Gideon stood there, looking less than impressed. "You ought to conduct yourself in a more civilized manner. This is grotesque," he said, taking the few steps down to where she was. "Get up."

Leona obeyed, though she was terrified. She didn't want to be anywhere near him. "What are you?" she whispered shakily.

Gideon smiled and tilted his head. "Come now, flower, surely you've worked it out by now? What about all those scary stories you love to read so much?"

Leona merely stared at him, afraid to say the wrong thing.

He approached her, his magic keeping her in place. Bringing his hand up, he gently wiped some droplets of blood from her lips. Leona flinched at the touch. "You are such a beauty. I did well in choosing you. You will make for a fine immortal."

"Immortal?" she whispered, her eyes wide.

"Vampire, immortal, whatever you choose," he said dismissively. "Monster, demon, creature, the list goes on. The humans are rather creative with their names," he chuckled. "We need to go over some things first. I can smell your hunger though, and I know you won't pay attention to me before you eat, so... let's get that out of the way."

"Why did you do this to me?" she asked, tears brimming.

"I did this for *you, flower. Don't you see? We can be together*

forever now, just like you wanted. We'll never be apart. And now you can use the true potential of your body. We'll exist together for the rest of eternity. I'll show you how to make the most of your immortality."

As she stared at him, a million thoughts raced through her head faster than she'd ever experienced before. She felt the most intense, paralyzing fear in her life, but it was covered with a thick blanket of... comfort. It was almost as if someone — or something — was trying to distract her from her true feelings. It was a pull unlike any other, one she couldn't help but bend toward.

Gideon's fingers were ice cold. Had she never noticed before? There had been times when they'd held hands that he'd been cold, but... God above, it was December! They were all cold. Weren't they?

Her emerald eyes roamed over the demon in front of her. The more she thought about it, the more she realized she didn't know him at all. She had been glamoured by his fancy words, his nice clothes, his pretty face, his smooth voice, even the way he smelled beckoned her closer. He had always been dressed up in suits, buttoned up to the neck. Perhaps she just hadn't had a chance to touch any of his skin before. But then again, she wouldn't have cared if he was as cold as he was now.

How could she have been so blind? Every time he had insisted on visiting her in the night, she thought it was just some romantic gesture so they could steal a few kisses under her father's nose. But now...

Her eyes were wide with both realization and terror. He wouldn't hurt her.

Would he?

"Okay," she eventually said, her voice wavering. "I… I trust you."

Lie.

"Good girl," he purred. "Let's get you changed and cleaned up. I'm going to show you how to hunt."

"When do I get to see my parents again? What about the wedding?" Leona asked in the early hours of the next morning.

Gideon peered up from the book he was reading. "What are you talking about, flower?"

"The wedding. My parents," Leona repeated. "Are we still getting married?"

Gideon shut the book and chuckled, folding a leg over the other. He was lounging in an armchair. They had just gone to feed and Leona had taken down two full-grown men, much to his surprise. She would be a fighter. "I'm not sure you understand what's happening, sweetheart. You will never see your family again. I have already arranged a messenger to send word to them that you've died in a riding accident. The wedding is not happening. Your family will mourn you, and in a few decades, everyone you know will be dead. It's the way of the world."

Leona was horrified. "What?" she whispered. "I… I never get to see them again? I'm not dead. I'm alive. I'm right here."

"Put your hand to your chest," Gideon said. She obeyed. "Do you feel a heartbeat?" he asked. At her silence, he tilted his head. "You are not alive. You aren't dead either. You are reborn. That's the new life I gave you, my sweet. Aren't you thankful? You will forever be beautiful, forever young, forever untainted. You will not fall ill, you will never get harmed by silly accidents, you will never be hot or cold. You can see the world as I see it, in every form it decides to take on."

"But…" Leona trailed off, her lips pursed in thought. She stitched her eyebrows together and looked at him. "What about a family? Our family? Our children?"

"Children?" Gideon repeated, then replaced that with a chuckle. "My dear, have you not listened to a word I have said? Those are mere mortal whims and desires. We do not have children. We cannot. Our organs no longer work as theirs do. Ours are improved. Better. Are you understanding me? I know you are not stupid."

Leona flushed in embarrassment. She always hated being belittled. As a beautiful woman, it happened more often than not, and she flared up every single time. "You killed me."

"Killed you?" Gideon scoffed in sheer amusement. He was shocked she was so standoffish about this. "I saved you, Leona. Surely you can see that."

"You killed me," she repeated, angrier this time. "You're a monster. You… You ended my life. You took my life from me. I wanted to marry you, raise a family, live happily ever after…"

"This is your new happily ever after," Gideon interrupted. "I'd think you'd be more grateful all things considered."

"Grateful?" Leona laughed in disbelief. She stood up and glared at him. "I am leaving."

"Careful," Gideon said, slowly rising to stand. "My patience only goes so far, darling. You don't know what you're saying. I know what's best for you. I can teach you everything. You just have to trust me."

"Trust?" Leona said. "Trust?!"

"Yes," he said. Leona ignored him and moved to leave, but he was quicker. He grabbed her and shoved her up against the wall, pictures rattling down to the floor with shattered glass. "Listen to me," he said in a low snarl, the glamour on his eyes fading. What was once a dark blue faded into a sinister red. She was frozen. "I am your master. You will refer to me as 'sire,' and I will protect you. I will nourish you, watch over you. You are to be my mate, Leona. I'll not tolerate your insubordination. Do you understand me?"

Silence.

He tightened his hold on her, causing her to cry out in pain. "Do you — understand — me?"

"Y-Yes," she squeaked out.

Slowly, he released her. Backing up a half-step, he stared down at her. "Never disobey me again. Never try to leave again. Or you will regret it."

Sebastian's gaze returned to himself and he came back to Earth. His body was still quaking and his cheeks, thighs, and top of his shoulders were all soaked with tears. Leona's face was that of somber defeat, like a racehorse that had finally been whipped into submission and broken.

"It only got worse after that," Leona said sadly. She hadn't wanted to overwhelm him. "When I left the first time, it was a few decades after he turned me. I had grown close to Piper and Whitney. They helped me escape. We ran away, as far as we could come, to this city. As I told you, everything was different. I thought I'd start fresh. How stupid and naive I was," she laughed bitterly. She had a faraway look in her eyes and Sebastian knew she wasn't there with him. "Damien led him to me. It was revenge against Whitney at the time. Theodore tried to shield me, keep him at bay, but nobody can stop Gideon from doing what he wants to do. He came and forced me back with him. When we got back to England, he locked me away for a decade. All I had were rats to feed on. When he deemed me fit for leaving my cell, he would rape me over and over, until I was begging him to stop. Then he'd throw me back in. People think they know what Hell is... they have no idea. Death was so tempting.

"It took Whitney years to convince Damien to let her in. Gideon was off traveling, learning of new medicines the humans had begun creating. He also heard whispers of a tribe of our kind in the Amazon. He is always looking for additions to his clan. While he was away, Whitney came, Piper in tow, and we ran away again. We didn't come back here, we stayed in Greece. It was hard. I was terrified the entire time, for decades. He found me eventually, all on his own.

"The bond between sire and fledgling is... intricate and intense. As I told you, the only way to break it is through death. He has killed his own fledglings before. He has made me watch, threatening that this will be my fate if I dare to defy him. If only I could be so lucky," she huffed. "I learned long ago that he will never let me die. I exist as an example to others, a demonstration of his power. He enjoys seeing my pain, inflicting it. A thousand years won't be enough punishment," she said. "The second time he took me back was worse than the first. He physically abused me, beyond rape. He would beat me, to the point where I felt like my chest was concaving and I would suffocate, despite my lungs being inoperable for two hundred years at that point. He would threaten my friends if I tried to go. He would threaten to drag them in front of me and skin them alive. Slowly burn them until their screams were the only thing I could hear in my deepest nightmares," she said with a shallow whisper. "I was too scared to retaliate for a long time. I resigned myself to this life.

"Piper helped me escape. Again. I still think we got away too easily. I believe it's a long game Gideon is playing. His showing up here proves just that. He's never *really* allowed me to escape. But… several months ago, Piper told me of some friends she met in Spain. Friends that could help us if turned. Friends that could… maybe be enough to end this."

Sebastian regarded her thoughtfully. It changed his perception of everything. "Do Charlotte and Victor know this is your purpose for making them immortal?"

"We were going to wait… but Gideon has sped the timeline along. I imagine Piper and Whitney are briefing them on the situation just as I am doing with you right now."

He frowned and felt conflict deep in his heart. "This isn't their fight."

"No, it isn't. But it's the price of entry to our coven," she said. "We all exist with targets on our backs as long as Gideon is alive. Whitney and Damien's relationship is volatile and, as you've seen, proven costly to our safety."

"Why doesn't she break up with him?" Sebastian asked. "If it's so dangerous."

"They're mated, Seb. It's not so simple. It's similar to my bond with Gideon. Though… I believe somewhere, Damien does truly love Whitney. I can see his loyalty to Gideon waver when she is threatened. It's the only reason we haven't killed him yet," she admitted. "And because it would destroy Whitney in the process."

"Would she die as well?"

"No. Not necessarily. But I can't do that to her," she said. "She is one of my oldest friends. She has put her life on the line for me more times than I can admit. It wouldn't be right. As I said… Damien is who she chose. I must respect that."

Sebastian frowned and shook his head. "Doesn't make sense," he muttered. "Why are they so cruel? You, Piper, and Whitney are not that way."

"We are different than some others of our kind. We believe living with humans can be feasible. Others merely look down on them. Predator versus prey. We don't want to be that way. At least I don't," she said. "I want to be normal. I want all of this to go away. I want you to be safe."

Sebastian looked at her, feeling a cross of anger and compassion for her situation. He hated he got dragged into this, but there was nothing he could do about it now. He knew his friends would turn eventually. And they would probably die trying to protect him.

It was almost enough to change his mind about immortality.

Almost.

"Do you think he will come back tonight?" Sebastian asked.

"No," she said. "But I don't think it will be long. I'm so sorry I've involved you in this. My selfishness clouded my judgment."

Sebastian shook his head. "I could have walked away. I could have said no, distanced myself from the situation. I didn't. I'm in this now," he said. "For as long as that may be."

"He'll kill you—"

"I'm not afraid of dying, Leona. I've faced death all my life. I've faced men who step on women they view as lesser beings, too. I made peace with death a long time ago. If I die, I die. If it's by my own hands, so be it. If it's by another's, alright. But dying for something worth fighting for? That's worth it to me," he admitted, placing his hand over his chest. "You deserve your chance at a normal life. At happiness. That's what I want for you. I want you to go through life without fearing that someone will take everything from you. I want you to laugh with your friends, to enjoy this never-ending story that's being written as we speak. You are worthy of love, Leona. You are worthy of all the things you dream of. No man, monster, or being, no matter how powerful or ancient, deserves to take that from you."

Leona stared at him, growing emotional all over again. She brought her hands up to hold his face yet again. This was what she'd been looking for all her existence. Those words were something she'd been yearning to hear for three hundred years.

"You make me feel alive again," she whispered, a few tears

rolling down her cheeks. Slowly, she pressed her forehead against his, his warmth seeping into her. Leona's fingernails gently trailed into his hairline, and she held him close, as if he would disappear in an instant.

"I love you, Sebastian."

16

Sebastian blinked a few times, those four words ringing in his ears. Silence hung between them as they stared at each other.

"What did you just say?" he whispered.

"I love you," she repeated. "All of you. I love your tender heart, your gentle mind, and that you look at me like I'm not a monster. You treat me as if I'm whole and not broken. You're willing to lay down your life for me, an immortal. An immortal that you haven't even kissed," she laughed quietly. "Perhaps I am just a fool in love, but—"

Sebastian leaned forward, cutting her off with a kiss.

Leona made a small noise of surprise and pleasure, her arms snaking tighter around his neck. She weaved her hands in his hair and returned his kiss, a few tears pricking her eyes. When they broke apart, his lips were red and puffy, and his cheeks were flushed. She rested her forehead against his again and gently massaged his scalp where she held it. "That's one way to do it."

"Now we've kissed, so everything else has to make sense," Sebastian whispered against her lips, his arms still holding her close to him. "Nobody has ever said that to me before."

"What? 'I love you?'" She asked. At his nod, she smiled sympathetically. "You are easy to love, Sebastian."

He snorted and shook his head, pulling back from her. "You'd be the first to make that assessment."

"What?" she repeated, turning to sit fully on the bed. She watched him get up to pace and felt her heart break for him. What had this man been through? How dare anyone make him feel anything less than beautiful? "I have seen every type of man in the world, both sinister and pure. They pale in comparison to you. I have loved you since the moment I laid eyes on you. There is a reason I was drawn to you. This was it. I was meant for you. I have waited three centuries to find you. I just didn't know where to look. Or when."

Sebastian ran a hand through his hair, his stomach turning with butterflies. More like an entire zoo. "Is that was this is, then? Love?" he asked, turning to face her. "Is that why I'm so afraid of losing you? Why I can't bear the thought of another man breathing in your direction? Of *possessing* you?"

Leona stood and approached him, closing the space between them. "Is that how you feel?"

"Yes," he whispered, their lips a hair's breadth apart.

"Then that's what this is," she said, her eyes hooded. "Does that frighten you?"

"Yes," he repeated. "Say it again."

She hesitated, then understood. A small smile crept

through her. "I love you."

"Again."

"I love you, Sebastian Beliveau."

"Again."

"I love you," she said, kissing one cheek. "I love you." The other cheek. "I love you." His nose. "I love you." His chin. "I love you." His forehead. "I love you," she whispered, finally kissing his mouth. Sebastian crouched slightly to meet her height, his hands trailing her hips. Their kiss grew hot and heavy, their tongues dancing together. His breathing hitched as she pressed the length of her body against his, their forms meshing perfectly together. They became one.

"Leona," he murmured, breaking their kiss for a painstaking moment. "Leona," he said again, interrupting her distracted and insistent kisses.

She looked up at him, fear flickering in her green eyes. She resigned herself to disappointment, knowing he would end this before it even began.

"I love you, too," he said, his fingers curling into her back.

It was Leona's turn to blink in shock. She tilted her head, her eyes wide with curiosity. "What?"

"I—"

"You do?"

Sebastian smiled and rolled his eyes. "As if I had any other choice, you temptress. You set your sights on me and that was that. Why do you think I ran away so much?"

"Because you didn't want me to drain the blood from your body."

"Mmm…" he hummed in amusement. "*Other* than that."

"You're just saying that to sound suave and romantic," she giggled, nudging his chest.

He caught her hand and brought it up for a gentle kiss. "I never just say things, honey. There is meaning behind every word. Every syllable. I. Love. You."

"Again," she teased, her gaze turning from bewildered to smoldering.

"I love you," he repeated, his kisses starting to trail from the top of her head down her face.

"Again," she breathed, arching her back.

"I love you," he whispered, kissing down her neck. Suddenly, he regretted giving her more clothes to put on. "I love you," he repeated, smiling as she parroted him back and fully gave into his touch. His hands slipped under the baggy shirt hanging off her body, his fingertips ghosting along her icy skin. She whimpered softly, feeling as if he were melting a path straight to her core.

"Show me how much you love me, Sebastian," she breathed, her fingers knotted in his hair.

"Happily."

And then there was no more talking. For a little while, at least.

Though Leona could easily take the reins and lift Sebastian with one hand, she allowed him to be in charge. She *wanted* him to be in charge. Despite being oppressed nearly all her life, this was different. He wasn't doing this to exert power over her. He was doing this *for* her.

Sebastian slid his hands under the backs of her thighs and hoisted her up, her ankles locking around behind his hips.

Their kiss resumed, and Sebastian's growing excitement was becoming evident. He walked them over to the bed and set her down gently. Though he would love nothing more than to split her in half, they had time for that later. This time — the first time — was reserved for making love.

"I'm not going to break, Seb. I promise."

"Oh, I know. That's for later. Just… try not to break me," he laughed, kneeling on the bed with her.

"You seem like the type of man that wouldn't mind it a little rough," she giggled.

"You'd be correct. But our definitions of rough might be different," he murmured. He grabbed the ends of her shirt and pulled it over her head, abandoning it on the floor. This time, he did not look away. He drank in the sight of her body, which was, like the rest of her, completely flawless. Resting back on his heels, he merely admired her.

Leona practically wilted under his stare. She was confident in her body and had never had a problem with it, but for the first time, she wasn't being *leered* at. She felt truly seen and appreciated.

"You are radiant," he said softly, passion in his eyes glinting with both love and lust. "The sun has planted roots within you."

If she could have blushed, she would have. She wasn't used to such positive attention. "Your words are so sweet. So genuine."

"You deserve it," he said. He hooked his fingers into the sides of the boxers she'd put on earlier. Pulling them down, he revealed her lingerie again. He intended to take his time.

There was no rush.

"Allow me to pleasure you," Leona said, feeling slightly uncomfortable. Not anything to do with him, but she was not used to receiving pleasure solely for the sake of her own enjoyment. Her pleasure derived from her partner and his pleasure. She was not used to generous lovers.

"My turn will come," he reassured. "This is your time right now," he said. Sebastian crawled over her and pressed a few toe-curling kisses against her lips. "Lie back for me."

Leona did as he asked, settling against the soft pillows. It had been a long time since she'd properly laid in a bed. Certainly longer since she'd had sex in one. She peered down at him, watching as he began a hot path of kisses from her collarbones, down to each of her breasts, her nipples, then to her stomach, her hips, her legs. She had never felt so *warm* before, not since she was a human.

Sebastian peppered kisses along her supple skin, before catching the waist of her lace panties between his teeth. Slowly, he tugged them down, crawling backward to get them off her legs. Taking them out of his mouth, he dropped them to the floor to join her other clothes. Once she was completely on show for him, he *really* took her in. His eyes roamed over her, to her center, and he suddenly felt parched. He had never wanted another person so badly before.

Before Leona could protest his actions, Sebastian's head was buried between her legs. Her jaw fell open and her eyes widened in both shock and some of the most intense pleasure she'd ever experienced. Instinctively, her hands found their way into his hair, keeping him in place. The feeling of his tongue against her was expert, and something she suddenly wished she had been doing for the last few centuries. It also proved to her what lousy lovers she had endured throughout her life. They expected this of her, but never returned the favor. He was doing it like he *enjoyed* it. He was licking her as if it were the last time he'd ever get to do *anything*. She tightened her grip on his hair, fully giving in to how wonderful his mouth was.

Sebastian made a slight noise of discomfort and eventually winced. He stopped and cut his eyes to her. "Leona, can you — loosen your grip just a bit," he managed to say, his eyes squeezed shut in pain.

"Oh! I'm so sorry," Leona gasped, immediately letting go. "Are you okay? I got a little carried away."

"No, I'm glad you got carried away. That was my intention. I'm fine, I promise," he said. "I just didn't want you to have a bald boyfriend."

Leona laughed heartily and rubbed his scalp for good measure. "I'd love you in any form. But your hair *is* really nice."

"Mhmm…" he hummed with a slight smirk. He lowered his head and his tongue flicked out again, killing anything else she was going to say.

Leona closed her eyes and opted to curl her fingers into the sheets. Her nails pierced the mattress and she felt her body building to a crescendo. She moaned his name, begging him for more, more, *more*. Then, her vision exploded into a galaxy of bright stars. Warmth flooded over her in waves, and she felt as if she'd just been reborn into nirvana. When he lifted his head, she couldn't look at him. She was afraid she was going to pass out.

Sebastian wiped the moisture from his lips, savoring the taste of her. He knelt between her legs, settling his hands on his thighs. "You are delicious."

Leona laughed and finally opened her eyes. Her fangs were fully extended after her climax. Pleasure was overtaking her like a ton of bricks. "That was... You're..."

"Wow, speechless. I am flattered," he teased. His hair was disheveled from her grip earlier. He looked down between her legs and smirked. "Shall I go again—"

"*No*, Christ," she said, putting her hand up to stop him. Her other hand fell over her face in embarrassment as she gave some smug giggles. "Nobody has ever done that before."

"What? Made you come?"

"No. Well... yes, but—" she stammered, shaking her head. "With their mouth."

"You've been alive for three hundred-something years and nobody has ever eaten your pussy?" he asked incredulously. As she shook her head, he frowned. "Well, no wonder you were such a bitch when we met."

Leona cackled and pushed herself to sit up. "You are *so* romantic in bed, do you know that, asshole?"

"I return that compliment to you," he grinned. "I'm still fascinated by how your body works."

"If I were you, I wouldn't spend too much time dwelling on the mechanics of everything. I've yet to figure it all out," she said. Her eyes roamed down his body and settled on the bulge between his legs. "Is it your turn now?"

Sebastian shrugged, trying not to sound *too* eager. "If you want to."

"Oh, fuck off," Leona laughed. She grabbed him quickly and turned them around, shoving him down into the mattress. Crawling to straddle him, she took hold of his shirt and ripped it in half. He might have wanted to take things slow, but she was in no such mood. She pulled the tatters off his shoulders and shoved them aside. Gently, she ran her hands up and down his chest, finally getting a good look at him. He was lean, his shoulders broad, and completely mouthwatering. Thin, dark hairs were scattered along his chest, and a thin patch trailed from below his navel and disappeared in the waistband of his pants. She could feel herself salivating, her teeth bared. She would love nothing more than to devour him—

"Leona," he said, catching her attention. "I'm going to be really upset if you drink me before fucking me. You can *at least* do me that courtesy."

She smiled and shook her head, her hair bouncing prettily on her shoulders and down her back. "Silly man," she whispered, before continuing her quest of undressing him. She untied the strings of his trousers, then pulled them down his legs once they loosened up. His boxers tented underneath, and she felt like she was going to explode with desire. Gently, she ran her hand over his length, teasing him through the material of his underwear. He groaned in delight and she felt like fireworks lit within her. She didn't have anything up her sleeve as unique as pulling his boxers down with her teeth, so she treated them the same as his shirt. Ripping them in half, he hissed under his breath as the waist pulled harshly against his skin before snapping. His cock sprung forward and Leona wasted no time in caressing it.

Sebastian jolted slightly and brought his hand down to cover hers. "I admit I am worried about your fangs near my dick."

Leona looked at him and opened her mouth, willing her fangs to recede. "It happens when I'm overly excited. I'll make a conscious effort to keep them hidden."

"You don't have to keep them hidden. They're a part of you. I just don't want you ripping me apart. I can't fuck you anymore if you do that. It's a lose-lose situation."

She laughed under her breath and nodded. "Noted. But I've done this a few times, Sebastian. I won't hurt you."

"Talking about other men during our sexy time. Nice."

"Asshole," she sighed, shutting up his next sarcastic retort by taking him in her mouth. She bobbed her head up and down, and now it was Sebastian's turn to hold onto her head. She appreciated that he didn't guide her in any particular way, or force her head down. He trusted her, and she was going to ensure he was rewarded for that. She flicked her eyes up to look at him, which was nearly his undoing. Sebastian held her eye contact and knew he would never get the sight of her between his legs, looking up at him like he was the only man in the world, out of his head.

After a few minutes, Sebastian slowly forced Leona's mouth off him. His chest was heaving and splotchy with how much blood was pumping through him.

"Was I not any good?" she asked in concern. Usually she had no issues making men finish.

"You were *too good*," he panted. "I'm afraid that this would end before it even begins. I also didn't know how you felt about where I should finish. I didn't want to assault the back of your throat."

Leona smiled and crawled back up to straddle him, her core teasingly rubbing against his length. "How very thoughtful of you. For future reference, I'll happily swallow every drop if it's from you."

Sebastian let out a shaky breath and nodded. "Noted," he quietly said.

Leona pulled him up by his arms until their chests were pressed together. She draped her arms over his shoulders and kissed him hard, tasting herself on his tongue. She rocked her hips against his, moaning into his mouth. His hands and nails raked down her back, trying to alleviate some of the pressure budding within him.

"I know I asked you to show me how much you love me, but I also feel like you deserve to be fucked after how brave you were tonight. What do you think?" she whispered into his ear, her lips trailing the outer shell.

Sebastian had died and gone to heaven. He buried his head into her neck, inhaling her. "I think that sounds very fair," he breathed.

"Good boy," she cooed, nipping his earlobe. She lifted up on her knees slightly and with his help, sunk back down onto him. They both hissed in pleasure as she seated herself on his lap, then began to move. She rolled her hips against his, their kiss never-ending. Her breasts pressed against his chest, their hands wandering over every inch of each other. Sebastian's legs bent slightly and he met each of her movements. Her hair curtained around them and it was taking everything in his soul not to explode.

"I love you," she whispered into their kiss, her voice heightened with pleasure. "I'm yours."

Sebastian felt tears burn behind his eyes. This was everything he never knew he needed. "I am yours," he repeated. "I love you in every world. In every century. In every way. I love you in eternity."

Leona let out an emotional cry, feeling overwhelmed. Her orgasm ripped through her, her body feeling like beams of light were piercing every part of her. She shuddered against him, which triggered him to go plummeting off the edge of ecstasy. Sebastian gripped her tightly, his roar of pleasure muffled as he bit her shoulder hard.

They stayed together as one for some time, neither of them moving.

As he held her, her body wrapped in his, Sebastian knew that loving her in perpetuity and his life could never coexist. He knew he couldn't have both.

He chose love.

eona stared at Sebastian as he slept peacefully. The worry lines that usually graced his features faded in the moment. The sound of his even breathing was the only thing in the room. She was hungry, and needed to feed, but didn't have the heart to leave him at that moment. She didn't want to risk him waking up and her not be there.

He had given her the greatest night of her existence. After the first time, they had done it a few more times, and she had come undone *every* time. She viewed intimacy differently now. Before, it had been a means to an end. She had never experienced sex as a human, only as an immortal. And even then, pleasure hadn't been her priority. Gideon was a selfish lover, and the men she took after him were all the same. She had always been told that the woman's pleasure came second, that she existed solely for the benefit and amusement of the man. Last night had completely opened her eyes. Would it be like that every time? Was it *supposed* to be like that? She hated assuming the worst of Sebastian, but she wouldn't blame him if he reverted to the stereotype she'd built in her head for men.

However, she knew he wouldn't. He never would. He shattered the mold.

Her eyes focused on him in the darkness. She was truly blown away by his beauty. He was different than past partners of hers. He was unassuming, humble, and endearingly awkward. She would have never guessed he'd be so commanding, yet generous in the bedroom. Mixed with his sweet nothings were some of the dirtiest, most erotic things she'd ever heard uttered. In one breath he'd be demanding she tell him what she wanted, and in the next, he'd be begging her for his own release. It was a give and take of emotion, one she had an equal part in.

That's what this was. Partnership.

She frowned to herself and reached out, gently running her fingers over a dark bruise that had formed on his arm. They had gotten a little carried away and she knew she hurt him, but he kept saying it was fine. Now that his body had a chance to recuperate, she could properly see the damage she'd done. It made her stomach turn, and she was suddenly disgusted with herself. This man was everything to her and she'd hurt him, all while she'd felt nothing but mind-numbing pleasure. It reminded her that their union was unnatural, and she had no clue how it would continue. He didn't want to be like them, and she respected that. Her last shred of selfishness longed to turn him, make him immortal so they could spend the forever and a day longer together.

Sunlight eventually bled through the cracks of the

shuttered windows. She stared at the rays, the little dust particles highlighted within them. How she *yearned* to feel sunlight again. She had always wanted to go to the coast, to a pretty beach somewhere. Or perhaps tanning on a boat. Or a nice stroll on a hot summer day. She looked back at Sebastian, feeling, *smelling* life on him. She wanted to let him sleep, but she couldn't help herself. Gently, she pressed a few kisses to each bruise she could find.

The man stirred and blearily opened his eyes. A sleepy smile spread through him as those familiar green eyes came into view. "Morning," he mumbled groggily, his hand immediately reaching out to rest against her hip. "I'd ask how you slept, but…"

Leona smiled. Always so sweet. "How did *you* sleep?"

"Good," he sighed, stretching out his body. The hungry look he received from Leona did not go unnoticed. "I'm sore," he groaned, before sitting up. He twisted his back a little, then got up to go to the adjoining bathroom. When he did, he caught a glimpse of himself in the mirror. His eyebrows shot up and he ran his fingers over his body. Dark bruises and scratches littered his skin. They varied in shape and size: some were like fingers where she'd held onto him, some were her clawing down his skin as she came, some were just them embracing. He looked like he'd gone ten rounds in a boxing ring and lost every time.

Leona was behind him swiftly, a sad, despondent look on her face. "Are you angry with me?"

"Why would I be angry?" Sebastian asked, turning to look at her. "Because of the marks?" She nodded. He smiled and shook his head. "No. I'm pretty sturdy," he teased. "Shows we had a good time, I think. Judging by you screaming the walls down so much that I'm sure I can never make eye contact with my elderly neighbor again…"

Leona sighed and shoved him gently in the chest. "Not funny."

"I promise, I'm okay. I know what I signed up for. I'm still alive, so I count this as a success," he said, before resuming his journey to the toilet. Leona grimaced and turned away from him. He looked over at her and scoffed. "I have had my tongue in every hole on your body and *this* is where you draw the line?"

"Just because I love you does *not* mean I want to see you piss," she said, busying herself with starting the shower up.

"Whatever," Sebastian said. "I better acquire at least two more bruises by the end of this shower."

"I'll see what I can do."

"Jesus! Sebastian, what happened to you?! Did Gideon find you?" Victor asked in concern as Sebastian and Leona walked into their home. They had tried to contact them, but hadn't been able to reach them. Piper had suggested against going to his house, just in case.

"Oh, no," Piper said with a knowing smirk. She was lounging sideways in an armchair, a glass filled with red liquid in her hand. "If Gideon had found them, Sebastian would be dead and Leona would be back in England. Those marks are something different," she laughed, tilting her head back.

"I don't understand," Victor said in confusion.

"They fucked, Vic," Charlotte muttered, before rolling her eyes.

"*Oh*," he said, then looked at his best friend. "All that for just one night of sex? What kind of freaky shit are you into?"

"Is bedding a vampire not freaky enough?" Sebastian teased, squeezing Leona's hand. His bruising was extensive, but it wasn't anything he couldn't handle. He was about as sore as he usually was after some rather rigorous exercise. He had assured her multiple times that morning that he was okay and would *gladly* repeat the process every night for the next 60 years.

"It's worse with werewolves. Consider yourself lucky," Whitney said from the other armchair.

Sebastian made a face that caused both Piper and Leona to howl with laughter. Perhaps it was the pot calling the kettle black, but he wasn't sure he could be down with going to bed with someone who was half dog. But when it came to vampires mating with other supernatural beings, he supposed it wasn't as strange as he thought. Luckily, he'd never have to be faced with that choice.

"Well, now that we're all here, this is as good a time as any to tell you the news," Piper said, standing up. "Sebastian, perhaps you should sit down," she added, eyeing Leona closely. She knew what was coming.

Sebastian felt Leona's hold tighten on him and he looked at his closest friends. At their apprehensive expressions, a wave of nausea washed over him. "You've decided?"

"Yes," Charlotte said. "We're doing it tonight. The sooner the better."

Sebastian's eyes trailed to Victor and the blonde nodded. He couldn't help the impending sense of doom that settled into his bones. He didn't want to be in the same room. He didn't want to think about any of this.

"Seb," Leona said, sensing his unease. "Let's go take a walk in the garden, shall we?"

He followed her outside to the back. The feeling of her next to him was the only thing comforting him at the moment.

"What questions do you have?" she asked, looking up at him.

Sebastian stared ahead and plucked one of the hundreds racing through his head. "Does turning feel like the memories you showed me last night?"

"Yes, but worse," she admitted. "I don't think there's any real way to convey how that feels. It doesn't last forever. Then you don't feel much physical pain after that, unless you provoke someone strong enough to inflict that. The emotional pain going forward is really the only discomfort you'll feel. Or being out of control of your thirst."

"Does thirst work the same way as it does for humans?"

"Sort of. Your throat gets dry, yes, and your stomach feels like it usually does when it's famished. But you also have this sort of... craze take over. It's like your brain doesn't work and the only thing you can think of is killing. You start to feel like you're being ripped apart after long enough. Then you grow weak. I am intimately familiar with starvation after being with Gideon."

"How long until I get to see them again?"

"You're going to have to stay away from them for a little while," she explained, trying to keep her tone calm, soft, and reassuring. "But it won't be forever. They're going to be much better trained than I ever was. They'll be introduced into our world properly, we'll make sure of that. We will support them. When you turn someone, it creates a bond, as you know. But it differs. It depends on the relationship you have with the fledgling before. If you're closer to them, then it's much stronger — Gideon and me. But if you aren't as close, it's weaker, and doesn't affect either of you as severely. However, it's enough to still care deeply for them. Piper will likely change one and Whitney the other. It's good they have them in their corners. There are certainly worse alternatives.

"I wouldn't go back to how it was, Seb. I miss my family, I despise the way I was ripped from them; the way I was murdered. But... the life I've led so far is extraordinary. It brought me to you. Otherwise, I'd have probably died in childbirth or something equally as gruesome," she admitted. "As I told you, the beginning was horrendous. If I had been supported properly, maybe things would have been different. I was a delinquent. Gideon only ever encouraged my feral side. I had other vampires telling me I needed to calm down. That was one of the first times I truly realized that *that's* not the right way to make the most of this burden. Killing people and wreaking havoc didn't make me feel better. Charlotte and Victor will be taught that from the beginning. You know I'd never sugarcoat anything for you, Seb."

She knew this wasn't exactly making the situation better,

but honesty would be the most helpful right then. She could sense his tension, so she reached out and took hold of his arms, stopping him in his tracks. "Look at me," she encouraged, knowing he was angry. "This is a decision they made a long time ago, regardless of what's happening with us and Gideon. This is something they've wanted and have deeply committed to. Piper and Whitney wouldn't even consider this if they didn't feel that they were serious and understood the consequences. There's very little either of us could do to change their minds," she said. She fought back the tears as Sebastian pulled away from her. She *knew* he wasn't angry at *her*, but it still hurt nonetheless.

Hopelessness was the main emotion that was wracking Sebastian's body. She had tried to reassure him that they would still be his best friends, that they would still be as they were. He turned his back to her and put his hands on his hips, looking down at the ground. "I want you to know that I'm not against becoming like you because I don't like what you are. I love you. Every part of you. But I told you I don't fear death. I told you I made peace with it long ago. No matter how happy I am, those thoughts of despair creep in and consume me in some ways. When I die, I want to *die*. I want it to be over. But… I must admit that I face a dilemma I have been grappling with for several days. Eternal life with you would be the *only* selling point of this. But there's no guarantee that we *will* be together forever. What if someone — like Gideon — takes one of us away from the other? What if you find another person…" he trailed off, sighing sadly as she immediately took him into her arms and whispered reassurances that that would never happen.

"I love you more than anything. That love is eternal, whether I am alive or not," he said. The thought of leaving her alone in this world with *him* was just enough to tip him over the edge.

Leona stroked his hair and pressed a gentle kiss to his cheek. "Why don't you go in there and say goodbye to them?"

So he did.

18

Staying away from them was difficult for him, but Leona kept him company. Piper and Whitney were too busy training their newborns. Leona was also staying around Sebastian for protection. He didn't need to be left to be flanked by Gideon. Then again, he might not even come back until Sebastian had grey hair. He never operated on a timeline.

Leona watched Sebastian edit some pictures from his latest photoshoot. She had all but moved in with him, never wanting to be apart. She enjoyed learning things about his life: his work, his art, what he liked to do for fun. He had shown her some of his favorite restaurants and bars, and she had explained what those places *used* to be a hundred years ago.

"You have a great eye," Leona complimented with a smile from the bed.

Sebastian glanced over his shoulder from his desk.

"Thank you." He turned back to his computer. It had been hard to act normal when he knew his friends were immortal by this point. It had been nearly two weeks since he'd seen them. Leona assured him that this was for the best, and that they needed to adjust to their new thirst around humans. She would never put him in danger, and he knew his friends wouldn't want to hurt him. Or at least, the version he knew wouldn't. He didn't know how different they would be now.

Leona stood up swiftly from the bed and snagged her cup from the nightstand, before perching up onto his desk next to the computer. "Why don't we stay in and do something fun tonight?" she suggested, sucking a dark liquid up through her straw.

Sebastian eyed her drink, then shifted his gaze up to hers. "What were you thinking?"

"Oh, I don't know… something to take your mind off everything. A distraction," she sighed, her lips and teeth glistening crimson. "Perhaps one that involves little to no clothing."

Sebastian smirked and shook his head. "I'm flattered that I've reduced you to a one-track mind."

She shot him a smile and leaned forward, tilting her head to look at his photos. "I'll give you another hour of editing, I'll finish my drink, and then we'll decide what you want for dinner. I'm *quite* the cook."

"Baby," Sebastian said, his eyes glued to the screen. "You and I both know you're shit at cooking."

"I feel like I've mastered spaghetti at this point."

"'Master' isn't necessarily the word I would use."

Leona called him a crude name and hopped off the desk. She loved the back and forth between them. It was easy, even when they were teasing each other. She knew he was enduring a lot of inner turmoil at the moment, and she hated that there was nothing she could do to take it away. It was one of the few instances where she truly didn't know how he felt. Mourning her own life was one thing, but her family had been taken from her in other ways. They lived their lives the way they were supposed to, albeit with unnecessarily added trauma of losing a daughter and sister. They never had to watch her become a demon.

He swiveled in his chair and patted his thighs, Leona immediately straddling him. They were eye-level now, a position he adored. Her eyes were some of the most enthralling things he was happy to become lost in. She constantly assured him she had never used her powers to lure him into her arms, but with the way she looked at him, she didn't have to.

"I love you," she whispered.

A smile. He always smiled at those three words. And he always said them back, no matter what.

"And I love your little smile when I tell you that," she added. "It fills me with warmth."

"A smile reserved only for you," he said.

Leona leaned back in his embrace. "Were you serious that first night about nobody ever saying 'I love you' to you before? Surely your mum…?"

"No," he said, shaking his head. "She just wasn't affectionate like that. Dad certainly never said it to me."

"Victor? Charlotte?"

He shook his head again. "No. But I felt their love in countless other ways. They didn't have to say it. I just didn't realize how much it meant until I heard you say it. That's why I asked you to say it over and over. I never wanted to forget hearing it on your lips," he said. "You said you loved me the moment you laid eyes on me, but... when did you *really* realize you loved me? That it wasn't just lust?"

She smiled and pressed the gentlest of kisses to his forehead. Her hands stroked through his hair. She loved his hair. She could spend all day playing with it. "There were a few moments bundled into one. The way you made me laugh on our first phone call, the way you looked at me as if I were the sun itself when we met by the river, and when you told me you wouldn't let anyone touch me ever again. You were protective, but it wasn't overbearing. It didn't feel controlling or threatening. It just felt like I was loved."

"You were loved. You *are* loved."

"When did *you* realize you loved me?"

"When we went to the ball. Seeing the way your face lit up when I picked you up in a horse-drawn carriage. Seeing how you came to life at how the manor was decorated. You just seemed so *happy*. I felt like I was looking at Leona in seventeen-hundred. Not twenty-fourteen. Maybe it was the lighting, maybe it was my imagination, but I could have sworn I saw color tinging your cheeks. Your smile reached your eyes for once, and that's something I've been trying desperately to do ever since we met."

Leona felt her heart twist. How cruel the world was to give her such a wonderful, kind man, who would eventually be taken from her, one way or another.

"I have waited centuries for someone like you. For *you*," Leona said quietly.

"I'm just a blip in your timeline of eternity, Leona. When I'm nothing more than dust, you'll forget about me in time. I'm sure of it."

"How could you say that?" she asked, frowning at him. "You are the reason I *breathe*, Sebastian. Protecting you, loving you, it is the only thing that gives me purpose. Perhaps that sounds dramatic, but it is true. What good is eternal life if it's spent in misery? I would rather have sixty happy, blissful years spent showing you the love you crave so desperately, than go another million without laying eyes on you again. You are worth every turmoil I've endured. A life with you is not a blip. My life has not been a *life* until I met you. Our souls will be intertwined together in every universe, in every era, in every sense. Mine has yearned for you long before you ever graced this planet. It yearns no longer," she exclaimed. "I described myself as soulless for a long time. You have shown me that that is not the case. It was merely lost, searching for you in a dark abyss of despair. The moment I laid eyes on you, it was like I could finally interpret the map to my salvation that had been taunting me for so long. When our bodies are gone, our love will remain."

Sebastian nodded, his throat tight. Words would not adequately convey what he wanted to say, so he communicated with a searing kiss. Muffled moans were exchanged between them as they frantically grabbed for each other, their kiss deepening as every second ticked by.

The way her hands held him, *possessed* him, was enough to send him over the edge. He leaned forward in the chair, dipping her back, if only just to get a little less distance between them. He tilted his head back as she planted a hot trail of kisses down his cheek to his neck. He could feel her teeth teasing his skin. Slowly, he redirected her head so they were kissing yet again. Leona would never harm him intentionally, but he understood how things could get out of hand in the heat of the moment. It was her instinct.

"I have something for you," he whispered when he broke apart from her for air.

"Mmm, yes you do," she giggled smugly, rocking her hips against him.

"An *actual* gift," he said with a small laugh. He reached over and unlocked the top drawer of his desk. He pulled out a small, slender box. Leona rested back against his knees and peered down at the package curiously. He opened it up, revealing a shimmering ruby pendant attached to a gold chain. She gasped softly, and Sebastian pulled it out. As it dangled and glinted in the light, the pendant's contents shifted. A liquid. "This is my blood," he explained. "It is mixed with a substance that will ensure it doesn't dry out. You said you preferred gold," he murmured. "I cannot give you that piece of me. But I thought this would be a good compromise. I want to commit to you, but… not in *that* way. Will this be too tempting for you?"

"No," Leona said, carefully turning the pendant over in her hands. This man was so thoughtful. She had always respected his decision not to be turned, despite the thought of losing him killing her. She had already been selfish enough in falling in love with him. "It's perfect, Seb. Will you put it on me?" she asked, getting up from his lap. Turning, her eyes fluttered closed as his nimble fingers quickly fastened the jewelry around her neck. The second that pendant touched her chest, she felt even closer to him. She could *feel* his life right there with her.

"I know it will not create a bond that exists sometimes between humans and vampires in those parasitic relationships, but…"

"Our bond is stronger than anything blood could buy," Leona interrupted, turning to him. She looped her arms around his neck and pulled him down for a soft and slow kiss. "You are my everything."

"And you're mine."

19

Sebastian held his camera up, the moonlight bouncing off Leona's pale skin. She looked ethereal. Her skin was so fair, he could practically see the blue wisps of veins beneath the thin layer. For being undead and 'soulless,' as she claimed, she was full of life in her own way. How could he look at this woman and think she was anything other than perfect? She had a brain, she had thoughts, words, ideas, opinions, blood, everything a human being had. Her abilities were just a little more enhanced, that was all.

"I feel silly," Leona laughed as she glanced back at him. "You'll make sure I won't look bad, right?"

"I don't think you *can* look bad, Leona," he reassured, closing the distance between them to show her some of the photos on his display screen. He scrolled through a few and looked over at her for her reaction. The smile on her face said it all. Relief flooded him. "See? What did I tell you?"

"You're so good at what you do. I wouldn't think this time

of night would make for very good photographs," she said.

"Well, not everyone is the badass photographer I am," Sebastian teased, turning the camera off and moving to set it down in his bag. They were in an expansive park in the northern part of town. It was after hours, but there was rarely anyone patrolling. If there were, they could easily slip away or hide. Or Leona could just... *persuade* them to leave them alone.

"You make me feel normal," Leona said as she sunk onto the blanket they'd brought with them. Their dates usually had to be at night, other than the odd stormy day when they could get away with being out in the late afternoon or evening. As long as the sun wasn't poking through the black clouds, she could operate comfortably. Otherwise... she'd be sore for days on end. "Sorry if you have to go out of your way to do anything with me. I'm sure it'd be much easier to be with someone you can go to the beach with or something."

"I hate the beach," Sebastian answered simply. He sat down next to her and crossed his legs, looking out toward the placid water the moonlight bounced off. "I hate most things, Leona."

"Is that so? I would have never guessed," she giggled.

"Apart from you," he added with a smirk. "Most days anyway."

Leona shoved him and Sebastian had to work to not topple over. He rolled his eyes at her cheeky apology, and he shifted to face her. "So... Other than your insane strength and smoking hot good looks... and your ability to influence how people feel and bend them to your will... What are your other powers? Do all vampires get the same ones?"

"Not necessarily," Leona sighed, thinking about her answer. How could she explain? "I wouldn't say I can read minds, but... like you said, I can influence how people feel. Some immortals do possess telepathy, and can clearly see into others' heads, but I just get a gut feeling on a general mood. I can tell when you're uneasy, unsure, scared, happy, excited, nervous. But I can't actually hear what your inner monologue is saying. Does that make sense?"

"Yes," Sebastian nodded. "I remember you sort of explained that during one of our first conversations. Anything else?"

"Is that not enough for you? Tough crowd," Leona teased.

"Come on," Sebastian whined, rolling his head back. "I'm just curious, that's all. Every time I think I know everything about you, you come back and convince me that there's *always* going to be something new to learn."

"Hmm... Okay, we can evanesce."

"You can *what*?"

Leona smiled and in a moment, she was a plume of black smoke. Sebastian jolted in shock and looked around. The woman was a mere few feet behind him, and quickly, she appeared behind him and wrapped her arms around his chest. "Evanesce. Teleport, to dumb it down for you. It takes quite a lot of energy and is very difficult. We can only go places we've been before," she explained, pecking a kiss to his cheek, before returning to her spot on the blanket.

"Wow... So you can go pretty much anywhere?"

"Something like that. It's easier to get around as an older

vampire. You've traveled more at that point. As a fledgling, you really only get to go places you've gone as a human. If you were well-traveled in your past life, then you've got a head start. I was not," she said. "Gideon took me a lot of places, showed me how to evanesce. It's quite an old talent, it takes time to master. There are some vampires who never quite get it. Or at least, can only travel short distances."

"What's the furthest you can travel?"

"Anywhere," she said. "Well, on Earth."

"Damn... I wanted to go to Pluto."

Leona laughed quietly and shook her head. "You'll have to find someone older than me then, I'm afraid."

"I draw the line at my women being three hundred, thank you very much. How old are you again?"

"Piss off," she snapped, folding her arms. "Any other questions?"

"Does it hurt? Feel weird?"

"It doesn't hurt, but it takes getting used to. It's almost like... when you suck in a breath and hold it. That feeling of just being frozen. That's all I can compare it to, honestly. You'd have to experience it to know what I mean."

"Can you evanesce with another person? Or will you just disappear and the person will stay where they are?"

"I can take people with me. Not a lot, but what I can carry. So you and maybe one other person."

"Cool," he responded. He hated to admit it to himself, but her abilities were a big selling point to being like her. He wasn't sure he could make that leap for teleportation and some added strength, but... it would be nice to be able to travel wherever they wanted, not worry about food, money, anything.

On the other hand, he would happily worry about those 'earthly' things rather than have to look over his shoulder for an ancient vampire trying to drag him back and enslave him. He felt horrible for her, and often wondered what went through her head daily. Did she think about it all the time? Even when she was with him?

"This is one of those instances when I can tell you're bothered by something. What's on your mind?" Leona asked, her eyebrows stitched together in concern.

"I was just thinking about Gideon," he admitted. "Couldn't you just evanesce away from him whenever he comes and takes you? Is that how you got out before?"

"That's complicated," Leona said. "Gideon... has this hold over me because he is my creator. My abilities are weakened when I'm around him. When I'm weak like that, it's very difficult to evanesce. If he's distracted or something, perhaps, but... the last few times he's stolen me, he made sure I was weak *constantly*. He wouldn't let me feed, he would keep his eye on me, sometimes I got thrown in his dungeon. It took Whitney and Piper breaking me out both times. I leaned on their strength. They don't have any physical or mental connection to Gideon, so his powers aren't as dramatic against them. He is still stronger than all three of us, but... if we're pissed off, we can at least wound him and distract him. It takes a distraction for me to even attempt to gather myself and do what I need to do."

"What's their story?"

"Whose?"

"Whitney and Piper."

"Oh," Leona said, pondering that question. "I've known them for a very long time, as you know. But as far as *their* background... It goes deeper. I met Whitney through Gideon, but she only knows him because of Damien. Piper is completely removed from our original coven. Though... we've made our own coven now, I suppose. Piper's very guarded about her past. I only know bits and pieces and I've known her for almost the entirety of my immortal life."

"Does that make it hard to trust her?"

"At first... yes. But she's stuck her neck out for me more times than I can count. I know she would die for me, and I would for her... in a heartbeat. Our bond goes deeper than just trusting each other. We're part of each other."

"And Whitney?"

"The same. You know you can ask them these questions. They won't bite."

"I'd rather ask you," he said. She was easier to talk to. Plus, he *knew* she'd tell him whatever he asked. He wasn't quite sure Piper and Whitney would be so forthcoming. And he was still pissed at them for changing his best friends, who he missed dearly. He didn't know when he'd be able to see them again, but Leona was doing a great job at distracting him. The only time he wasn't around her was when he was on assignments and shoots. She was never too far behind though. She often took that time away to go hunt and make sure she was safe for him to be around when he came back home.

"Fine... Who do you want to know about first?"

"Doesn't matter. But I want to know both."

"Okay... I can start with Piper. What I know, anyway."

1700.

"Piper, please! See sense!"

"No, Mother. This life is for you, not for me. I don't want to be part of all this pomp and circumstance. I want to travel, I want to see the world. I want to command ships and explore! I don't want to be cooped up in a home with some stuffy husband who only sees me as a breeding tool. I want to be more than just a body to him while he gets drunk and fucks mistresses. Didn't you want more with your life before all this?"

A young and vibrant Piper stared at her mother in the middle of their home. They were in England, near Liverpool, a place Piper had been all her life. She was in a pair of brown, dirty trousers, and a laced up, loose cloth shirt. Her mother was clad in a fine dress, her hair and makeup done immaculately. As usual.

"Adventuring is not a lady's place," Lady Aldene scoffed, shaking her head. "Where did I go wrong with you? The Aldene name is one to be proud of, and you just want to throw it all away... for what? For what, Piper? To go live out some fantasy in a world that will chew you up and spit you out? You are far too old to be fussy at this point. Before, you could have had any man in this world, and we showed you many suitable bachelors, but now... You'll be lucky if you get someone who holds any respect in the darkest corner of the world. You are soiled."

"I'm not soiled, Mother. I'm anything but. I'm alive. I'm alive,

and I want to be free. If that means dropping the Aldene name and making a new identity for myself, then so be it. But I will not be shackled to anyone, let alone some man who can't do anything but keep me on a rope. That may be satisfactory for you, but I won't stand for it. I'm going."

"Where? Where will you go, Piper? You'll be nothing without your father and me. Absolutely nothing. You're going to come crawling back here and we won't have you. If you leave, you are no longer our daughter."

"Fine," Piper said as she stormed upstairs to pack whatever she possibly could. A life of skirts, dresses, wigs, and makeup wasn't for her. She didn't want to sit around each day, knitting, cross-stitching, and gossiping with the other hens of the estate on who showed whose ankles to the stableboy. Minutes later, she came bounding down the steps with a bag slung over her shoulder. Without a passing glance or a goodbye, she set off out of the house, grabbed a knife, bow, and quiver on her way out, and went about her new journey.

A few years passed and she felt like she was thriving. She had traveled from country to country, not caring about money or where she would find her next meal. Gone was the good girl brought up by the Aldene family. Here she was, just Piper, and nobody could ever take that away from her. She drank what she liked, fucked whom she liked, ate what she liked, and lived where she liked.

There were whispers of some faraway land that existed across the vast ocean where people were settling, but that seemed like a dream to her. She had always believed the world to be a plane, but the stories the historians told suggested otherwise. Surely all those people couldn't be lying about this new place? This new country to start fresh?

In her curiosity, she had booked a ship that was rumored to be exploring further than anyone had ever gone before. She hadn't enough money to commandeer her own fleet, but that was of no consequence to her. She had her sailors and she had plenty of training behind the mast of a ship. Men had taught her all sorts, men who respected her more than just for what her body had to offer them. She didn't trust any man as far as she could throw them, but... they certainly came in handy when she needed something.

However, a man wasn't who ended up slaying her. A woman, whom Piper only knew as Margery, bewitched her and caught her in her snare. Piper had become quickly infatuated, finally meeting a woman who shared the same sense of whimsy and adventure she did. They had talked about going on the ship together, seeing the world, finally knowing if these rumors were just that or actually true.

They bunked together below the deck and Piper gave in to all the feelings she'd had her entire life. She felt alive, like everything had finally fallen into place. A woman who loved her for her, exactly as she was, and they could do life together.

Until one night, while Piper was asleep, Margery took her opportunity and infected the blonde. The change hadn't taken long, a few hours at most, and Margery explained to Piper when she woke that she was to be her apprentice; that she was 'exactly what she was looking for' and things would be better, different that they were together.

"Doesn't that sound nice?" Margery said with a smile. "You and me. Like we said."

"Is that all you wanted? An apprentice? Someone to teach?"

Piper asked, her voice raspy from the thirst overtaking her throat. "I wanted a partner. A lover. A wife."

Margery merely laughed in response, as if it were the most childish notion in the world. "Such mortal concepts. This is why you need a teacher."

"Why didn't you kill me?"

"I told you why. You don't listen, do you?"

Piper clenched her jaw, and in the next second, saw red. Using her newfound strength and rage, she ripped Margery limb from limb. The vampire had been caught off guard, not expecting such finesse from a new immortal. Piper's past experience learning how to fight as a girl had helped in this arena, and after a bloodied heap of woman lay at her feet, she knew that this new life was meant for her.

She was just meant to walk it alone.

Afterward, her thirst took over and she killed every man aboard the ship, sucking all of them dry. Worrying that Margery may somehow return, Piper purposefully sunk the ship near Balperro, and swam the rest of the way to land back home. It was bitterly cold, and she had hoped she might die on the way, but her abilities were tested and proven to be unwavering.

A few years later, she had been hunting, and had nearly killed a redhead in the process. She had been wary of trusting her, hints of Margery coming back to the forefront of her mind. But this woman was different. She was kind. She understood. She knew how this felt, to be alone, to be misunderstood, to be taken advantage of.

From then on, Piper made a silent vow to herself to always protect Leona. She was everything to her.

"Do you think she loves you?" Sebastian asked.

"Yes," Leona answered simply. "She does. She has told me. But the type of love she seeks from me, I cannot give her. We have long since moved on from it. But that doesn't mean I wouldn't do anything for her. All she needs to do is ask, and I will fulfill her request in an instant."

Sebastian nodded. Strangely enough to him, he didn't feel jealous. He just felt... *relieved* that she had someone like that in her life.

"Sounds like you know more than just bits and pieces about her life."

"Well... I suppose it depends on what your definition is. I don't know hardly anything about her mortal life before what I just told you. And as far as her adventures as an immortal before I met her, she has kept tight-lipped on that. I think she feels guilt for some things she's done. But we've all done terrible things. We all got better when we found each other."

"And Whitney? What about her story?" he asked, tilting his head.

"Her story isn't quite so... dramatic. Really, it's just her being a nosy parker."

1705.

Whitney scribbled down a few notes, glancing back and forth from her paper to the books open across the table she was sitting at.

She was a student at Oxford University, but this wasn't schoolwork. She had always been fascinated with the occult and the supernatural. Things that couldn't be explained. It was the only way to explain certain phenomena, in her opinion. Currently, her fixation was on immortal beings that drank blood and created covens of their own kind. Beings that lived in the shadows. There wasn't much literature on the subject, and these creatures didn't even have a name. But they were interesting. From the little legends she'd found, traveling to different parts of the country to speak to tribespeople, these monsters were charismatic, one of their predatory traits. They had a certain look, scent, and voice even that drew their prey in.

And their prey was human.

She had gotten some leads on what could possibly be one of these shadow-beings lurking near Ireland. It hadn't taken her long to follow the trail and document everything as she went. It took months to get anything substantial, and she had taken up some work to pay her way. This hyper-fixation was different than her last ones, purely because she felt like she was so close. She had abandoned her studies at the university to pursue this, much to her parents' and friends' chagrins.

But the stories people would tell about her when she finally proved she was right!

One night, she was wiping down the countertop inside the pub where she was a barkeep at. It was nearly time for her to go home, but something was pulling her to take her time with her closing duties. As she left, dumping whatever rubbish they had left from the night out in the back, she was stopped by a man asking for directions.

"A block that way, to your left. It's the building with the big iron gate."

"Thank you," the man smiled. "What's your name, darlin'?"

"Whitney. Whitney Blackwoode. And yours?" she asked, outstretching her hand.

The man gave a pretty smile. "Something much less gorgeous than that, I'll assure you," he answered, gently taking her hand. His skin was ice cold. "You're not from around here, are you?"

"No. Oxford," she answered. "Your accent isn't familiar to me. Where are you from?"

"Nowhere important," he said cryptically. "Have you heard all those stories about some monster killing people 'round here? Scary stuff."

"Yes," she said, lighting up. "I have! You have, too?" she asked. That meant these stories were making their rounds. Maybe there was something here for her to find. "They say it's a creature who lurks in the dark and sucks blood. I can't believe they don't have a better description than 'human-like.' Something like that would be hard to miss, I'd think."

"Maybe that's what makes this creature such a great predator. Can hide in plain sight. Maybe even sneak up on innocent girls who ask too many questions."

Whitney laughed nervously, but the sound died in her throat when she realized that it wasn't a joke and he wasn't laughing. Suddenly, fear overtook her, and for the first time in her life, she wished she'd never picked up any book on monsters in the dark.

"I'll make this worse for you if you scream," he said, and suddenly, she was pinned up against the wall. "Usually girls like

you aren't so interested in all this. What happened to making dresses and being a good wife?"

Whitney struggled, knowing that panicking would only escalate the situation. She had to pretend she wasn't scared, even if she knew he could smell the terror emanating from her. "Research is my husband."

The man barked out a laugh and raised his eyebrows. "Maybe I'll keep you around. We'll see. Maybe you'll bleed out."

"What are you going to do?"

"You know what I'm going to do, Whitney."

Whitney woke up later in a pool of her own blood. Everything was different, of course, and she knew then that she had been transformed by whomever that man was. She was everything she'd been searching for.

And she was determined to use this newfound power to find out even more, to find the good ones. There had to be some of those, right? There had to be ones that didn't prey on girls in the dead of night and scare them. She was sure he thought she would die then when he threw her away, else he wouldn't have let her live.

Not long after that, in her quest for knowledge, she met Damien Hawthorne, a beast who captured her heart. He, in turn, introduced her to a fellow immortal, Gideon, who introduced her to his new mate and fledgling, Leona.

After a while, she and Leona banded together, along with their newfound friend Piper, and swore to bring pain to anyone who hurt them. They would protect each other.

And so they did.

"Wow," Sebastian said, shaking his head, "Heavy shit. And definitely still just as dramatic. Should I even ask about this Damien dude?"

"Another story for another day. He annoys the shit out of me," Leona laughed, waving her hand dismissively. "He and Gideon practically feed off one another. It's maddening."

"Why does Whitney stay with him if he's so annoying and close to Gideon? Does that bother you?"

Leona shrugged. "It did at first, purely because I was afraid it would lead Gideon to me through their connection. Which it did, but Whitney feels bad enough about that. All things aside, who am I to stop her from loving who she loves? When she and Dame found each other, she didn't know what would transpire after that. I wish he treated her better, but… That's her cross to bear. No pun intended."

"Ha, ha," Sebastian deadpanned. It was quite a noble way of thinking. He wasn't sure he'd be quite so selfless. "So," he said, wanting to change the subject to something a little less depressing. "If I haul my bag with all my gear, can you evanesce us home? I'd rather not have to take the streetcar."

"I *like* the streetcar, though."

"I know you do, but… when you've ridden it your whole life versus getting to vanish in a puff of smoke… you have to understand which option I'd prefer," he said with a smirk.

"Simple minds, simple pleasures… Isn't that the saying? *Abrin.*"

"Oh, 'Abrin' is it, now? I'll remember that later when we get home and you're begging me to—"

Sebastian leaned forward and cut her off with a kiss. His

hands slid from bracing himself on the blanket, to her knees, up her thighs, and around her torso to pull her into him. After a few blissful moments of losing themselves in each other, he pulled back. *One* of them had to breathe, after all. "Begging me to... what?"

"Home. Now."

Leona grabbed his bag and him, and they were gone a second later.

20

"Ready, Sebastian?" Piper asked as she smiled at him. At his meek nod, he gestured for Victor and Charlotte to come out.

Sebastian slowly approached them. They didn't look that different. They had already been pretty much flawless, this was just amplified. They held themselves differently, but he could still see his best friends inside. "Are you going to try to kill me?"

"Not today," Charlotte giggled, before throwing her arms around him. "I missed you so much, Sebby!"

Sebastian groaned in immense pain, his legs nearly giving way beneath him. "Charlie... crushing... me..." he ground out, trying to get out of her grip.

"Sorry!" she said as she pulled back. "Not quite used to my new strength. Never been able to bring you down before," she laughed, poking his chest, which made him stumble back a bit. She quickly brought her hand back to her chest. "Sorry," she whispered whilst making a face.

Victor shook his head. "Can you tell she's excited?" he teased. "We're the same as we've always been, Bas. Just a bit less fragile."

"Mhmmm…" Sebastian hummed, before looking at Leona. How did he venture into a part of his life where everyone he knew was a vampire? What had his world become? He watched them closely; wondering how they would change and being faced with it were two very different things. Seeing them so *normal* made his head spin. They hadn't tried to attack him. They hadn't done anything out of the ordinary. It made him think about possibly considering…

No.

His internal monologue was constantly pulling an angel and devil on each shoulder act. It wasn't as if he had anything to lose at this point. He had no family, and his only two friends and girlfriend were part of the underworld. He would still be able to take photos and create art, and if he decided he wasn't suited for their lifestyle, Leona had told him there were ways to end vampires' lives.

It was overwhelming him. A couple of months ago, he would have never expected to be put in the middle of a potential vampiric blood-bath between an evil overlord and a woman whom he couldn't imagine being without.

Would it be so bad? To be like them?

"I'm sure you have a lot of questions. That's normal," Whitney said, looking at Sebastian as if he was about to run out of the door. "You know we won't hurt you, Sebastian. Or pressure you. This is for your protection. Nobody will touch you now that you've got five vampires as a security detail."

He had a hard time believing that, not when Gideon Valdis was out for his blood — literally. Folding his arms, he slowly sunk into a chair. "Have you been killing people?"

"Yes. Piper took us a few states away. Criminals, like they do. Bad areas, crime-ridden, where our presence wouldn't be noted as severely. Metropolitan areas are best and most inconspicuous," Charlotte explained. "It's a whole new world, Sebastian."

"Do you miss the sunlight?"

"Yes," she said, looking to Victor as he agreed. "But it's a small price to pay for the wonders we've experienced. They have shown us that we don't have to be cooped inside twelve hours a day. There are ways around the dangers of the light, as I'm sure Leona has explained to you. Things won't be that different, Sebby, I promise. We're still going to be here for you *always*."

Leona could sense that Sebastian wasn't listening too intently to what they were saying. It was a lot to take in, especially given how close they were to him. She gently placed her hand on his shoulder. "I'm sure they're both grateful for your respect in their decision. You are handling this well, Sebastian. Much better than most. I'm also sure that they will want to prove to you that their change was not a mistake."

It was too much all at once, despite knowing the outcome. It reminded him of his youth, when everyone else would have the shiny, new toys, and he'd be left behind with scraps. He had always been a misfit, even when being taken in by the Labasques all those years ago. This felt no different. Here he was, the only human in the group. It would be all too easy to change that, but he was still steadfast in his decision.

"I want to be alone with my friends," Sebastian said.

"Sebastian, maybe that's not the best—"

"Fine," Piper said, cutting Leona off. She looked at her pointedly and communicated, *Don't push it* without actually saying anything. The blonde, redhead, and brunette left the room. Sebastian knew they would probably be able to listen into their conversation, but he didn't care. He just wanted to be with his family at the moment.

"You both look like you," he said quietly. "What are your favorite parts about this change?"

Victor spoke first. "It has been a difficult adjustment, I'll admit. Finding things to do at night instead of sleep. Occupying your time. Hunting was quite an experience, one that was more daunting than I anticipated. But I don't regret it at all. It's just a whole new world. Or at least… my understanding of the world has been expanded. There's so much more for us to learn."

Charlotte nodded. "We're still us, Sebby. I promise," she said, moving to squat down next to him. Comfortingly, she took his hands in hers. "I appreciate you being so patient with this decision and respecting it. I know it's hard and I know you hate it, but… just trust that we know what's best for us. This is what's best for us."

"Can you evanesce? Leona said it would take a while for a new vampire to become properly trained, but that a well-traveled human would have a head start."

"We are learning. Charlotte is better at it than I am,"

Victor said, glancing at his wife. "She can go long distances, but I can't go quite as far yet. She carries me a lot of the way."

"Always better than you, glad that hasn't changed," Sebastian said with a half-hearted smile.

"Anything else you want to know? We want to answer all your questions," Charlotte reassured.

Sebastian shook his head. Honestly, his brain was swimming. There was so much happening, so much change… Things were different, they were different, but *not*. How long would it be until they moved on? Got bored of their pet human?

He felt like his mouth was full of cotton. There were so many things bubbling within him that died on his lips before they made it out. His abandonment fear was coming true, and eventually, everyone would be gone. Or rather, he would be. He would grow older and they would stay frozen in time. They would never get sick or get into some accident that took their lives. Would Leona grow bored with him when he turned grey? When he got wrinkles? When his skin started to sag? Would they all leave because he couldn't keep up with them anymore? Because they didn't want the same old, same old, and disappeared to find something new?

"Sebastian," Victor said, drawing him out of his manic daydream. "You're panicking. Stop it. Take some deep breaths," he said, squatting opposite of Charlotte. Sebastian stared at them, worried that if his chest constricted any tighter, it would concave and pop inside him. Victor moved closer to him and pulled him down onto the floor with him. "Lie on the floor," he said softly, making sure his face pressed to the cool stone below. "Breathe deeply. Just like I said. In… Out," he soothed, laying down with him. This wasn't the first time they'd done this together. Victor had learned how to handle Sebastian's anxiety when they were teenagers, and he had never left him alone in the middle of an episode. This was no different. "I'm right here, Bas. Right here. I'm not going anywhere. Not now, not ever. We made a pact, remember? We're brothers forever. Even into oblivion."

Sebastian focused on him, his vision going in and out. The cold floor was enough to ground him, and he could feel his chest loosening. Faintly, he heard Victor instruct Charlotte to get him some water and a cold, wet rag to press to his head. Victor stayed with him, just as he said he would.

Sebastian hated getting like this. He hadn't been this way since his parents died and he was worried he would go to prison for the rest of his life. Victor had calmed him down like this, but in his bedroom. They lay together and talked, worked on breathing, and leveled each other. It was one of the few moments they shared where Sebastian truly felt like he was magic.

"Let me know when you want to sit up," Victor whispered. After an age, he got up, the blonde reaching up to keep the compress against his forehead. Sebastian's black locks were damp and strung against his temples and cheeks. He was pale, but he was past the point of passing out. Looking up, Victor took the glass of water from Charlotte and handed it to his best friend. "Drink this. All of it. Okay?"

"Okay," he muttered, doing as he was told. He felt like a teenager again, and here was Victor, always to the rescue.

After downing the drink, Sebastian set the glass down on the floor with a clink. He leaned his head on Victor's shoulder and shut his eyes, the lids burning with exhaustion. His body sagged against him and he just started to cry. Charlotte joined them on the floor and held his other side, allowing him to let his feelings out.

Sebastian wasn't crying over their loss of life. It was much more than that. The fear he harbored about his own mortality was part of the mix, but he mostly felt relief. For the first time in this entire, insane situation over the last few months, he felt like things were going to be okay. He felt relief in that he could focus on the here and now, the *happiness* he'd been gifted with Leona, without fretting about her falling out of love with him. About his friends going away. About something wretched happening that would leave him isolated. His friends *would* be there for him. Leona *would* love him. Her words *were* true, and he was *okay*.

Slowly, he brought his arms up to clutch onto his friends' embrace. He considered it a win that they weren't crushing him with their brute strength. He smiled to himself at the thought and closed his eyes, a laugh rumbling from the bottom of his throat. "You two get changed into vampires and I'm the one that steals the show."

The couple both joined in his laughter. Victor shook his head and nudged him away. "You always were the dramatic one, Beliveau."

He opened his eyes and looked at them, his insides settling to their normal places. The fury and uncertainty in his stomach died down to a whisper — one he could ignore for a little while longer. He hoped for silence someday. The vampire trio emerged from the adjoining room, not wanting to encroach on their moment, but sensing the request for privacy had passed. Sebastian moved his gaze from his friends, to the woman he loved and *her* people. He was sure she felt scared to lose Piper and Whitney, just as he did with Charlotte and Victor.

We'll be okay, Sebastian thought. *No matter what.*

21

few weeks had passed since everyone in Sebastian's
life became an immortal. He was used to it by
now. They traveled as a pack at night while he
slept to feed, and Charlotte and Victor had even arranged
a partnership with local hospitals and blood banks. It was
beneficial to everyone. Nobody got murdered, the banks got
generous donations and funding, and they were supplied with
blood regularly. Leona had told him her favorite was AB-,
which both amused him and grossed him out.

The Labasques were very well-known in the community;
Sebastian had *no* clue how they were going to swing their
'deaths' eventually. Piper suggested they just move away after
several years and come back when everyone was dead. That's
what they usually did. Then nobody would know them. They
certainly had enough wealth to last an eternity.

Christmas and the new year had come and gone, and
everything was quiet as far as Gideon went. Sebastian's stress

consumed him sometimes, and he found it hard to sleep; luckily, Leona was always there to comfort him and keep him company when his insomnia spread through him. They stayed awake talking about all sorts: his childhood, some of his favorite memories in the city, her favorite places she's visited or lived over the last few centuries, and their plans for the future. Sometimes the conversation was difficult, especially when they were faced with the fact that one day, Sebastian would be gone and Leona would be left alone. It was difficult for him to reassure her because there was no getting around it.

Though, in the time he'd spent getting to know Leona, taking her out, making love to her, his resolve was slowly crumbling. His friends seemed to be adjusting to this new lease on life well, and he didn't necessarily *have* to kill humans if they kept this deal with the hospitals.

Leona still wore his blood pendant all the time. She never took it off. He had come close to letting her taste him several days ago, but he'd stopped himself. She had been respectful about it, and only her repetition of asking for consent made him come to his senses. He appreciated that she always triple-checked if he wanted something, instead of just going for it and asking for forgiveness later.

They had discussed possible contingency plans for if Gideon showed up out of the blue and wanted to cause trouble. Charlotte and Victor had been training with the girls, honing their skills and becoming comfortable in their new bodies. Sebastian often watched their sessions, which took place in the courtyard of Labasque Manor. They would spar, use their magical abilities, and test each other's limits. None of them possessed the great power Gideon did, but Leona, Whitney, and Piper were intimately familiar with what he brought to a battle. All they could do was bring a good defense, because they would *fail* in offense.

Sebastian sat on his porch, the sun beginning to set as he scrolled through his phone. Often, he would spend time alone in the sun or during the day while Leona rested or occupied herself in other ways. She had reassured him to continue enjoying parts of his human life, even though she couldn't.

She certainly relished in parts of her immortal life while he needed sleep.

"Coming in soon?"

At the sound of Leona's voice, Sebastian tore his eyes from his phone to glance at her. As he answered, he did a double take and sat up straighter. She was completely naked, showing off her flawless form. He almost dropped his phone. Her body was mouthwatering, and he was completely helpless to her womanly wiles every time she decided to distract him. He started to stand but was interrupted by a rather alarmed, high-pitched noise from nearby. His head shot to his neighbor's porch, where an elderly woman had her jaw dropped wide open, her dog beginning to bark.

"Go inside," Sebastian hissed as he gently pushed Leona behind the threshold. He lifted his hand in an apologetic wave to the woman next door. "Sorry, Mrs. Sodeko. Tell Pookie I said hello."

As he scrambled inside, Leona had her eyebrow raised. "Pookie?"

"I didn't name her dog!" he snapped, shutting the door

behind him. He wasn't angry with her — because that would be impossible in her current outfit. "I'm not complaining about your choice of attire *at all*, but we need to remember that things like that can send my seventy-five-year-old neighbor into cardiac arrest," he said with a laugh.

Leona rolled her eyes and pressed her body against his. "Perhaps I want to send *you* into cardiac arrest, Mr. Beliveau," she purred, moving her teeth to tug at his earlobe.

He let out a shuddered breath and grabbed her hips, before pushing her up against his bookcase nearby. She didn't miss a beat and hopped into his arms, her legs looping around his waist. Their kiss was animalistic and passionate, with tongues and teeth gnashing everywhere.

They varied back and forth on who dominated whom when it came to sex. Obviously, Leona was the stronger one of the pair, but she liked to put him in charge just as much as she liked *being* in charge. Sebastian was happy to let her take over when she wanted — in fact, he preferred it. She was always nervous in the back of her mind about hurting him, but as he'd told her, he was sturdy. He enjoyed the marks — he always told her it was the best reminder of her.

"Tell me what you want," Sebastian breathed against her, his lips brushing against her cheek and down to her neck.

"Fuck me," she barely managed, tilting her head back against the books. Were she a human, this would be vastly uncomfortable. But as a vampire, she hardly noticed it. Her nails dug into his neck as his hands fumbled below them to undo his jeans. Sebastian wasted no time and in a moment, he was sheathed deep inside her. Leona let out a guttural moan as she bit down on his shoulder, careful not to draw blood. She wasn't sure she would be able to control herself otherwise.

Every time they made love, the world seemed to stop on its axis. Sebastian always saw stars, his body lighting up with pleasure as her walls pulsed around him. She liked playing rough and as much as she marked him, he did his damnedest to return the favor. Of course, her skin healed quicker than the marks could even appear, but she *liked* the pressure of his teeth and fingers against her. It was always 'harder, faster, *more*.'

"I love you," Leona breathed, her words hitching slightly. "Right there," she continued, books rattling behind her. "Please, please, *please*."

Her demands rang in his ears, and he was a slave to her command. Pleasure shot through him like a bolt of electricity. This woman, who could splinter every bone in his body in an instant, was begging *him* for mercy in her ecstasy. His fingers curled around the back of her neck and he caught her lower lip between his teeth.

"You are *mine*, Leona Abrin. Mine," he growled against her lips, his hips still working furiously against her. The only sounds in the room were their bodies meeting, his lusty declarations, and the wood of the shelves clattering against the wall. "You will be ruined for any other *creature* after me. If you *ever* decide to find something else, you'll find yourself thinking of me. You'll look up at him and exclaim to a God you don't believe in wishing it were my name on your tongue. I will split you in half *every* time you ask and lick your wounds like a man starved. I'm yours and you're mine."

"*Yes*," Leona cried out, tears streaming down her cheeks with the jolts coursing through her veins. She had never longed for flames so much before. "I was in a tomb before you, my love," she said, sobbing with pleasure. "You resurrected me."

"In life, death, and whatever comes after and between, I will find you. My soul is embedded in yours and one cannot exist without the other," he breathed, feeling an eruption budding inside him. "Come for me, honey," he whispered against her lips. "Please."

That was all Leona needed for her orgasm to rip through her and turn her inside out. She dug her nails so deep into his back that she *did* break the skin this time, but her climax was so powerful that the scent of blood didn't even register. She moved her hands over him, up into his hair, tugging slightly. Sebastian had spilled himself deep inside her, his forehead pressed against her shoulder. His body heaved with the weight of his breathing. Fearing his legs would give way, he slowly set her back down on the floor.

Leona had not been out of breath in dozens of decades, but right then, she felt light-headed. She sunk down to the floor and rested back against the bookcase, books open-faced and bent all around her. She kept her gaze on him, and only in the afterglow of their lovemaking did she smell it.

"Are you bleeding?" she asked softly, her eyes hooded.

Sebastian frowned and brought his hand around his side to touch his back. When he looked down at his palm, he saw crimson spread across it. "Oh. I'm okay, don't worry. Are you—"

"I'm fine," she said, looking away from him. It was extremely tempting, but she loved him far too much to risk anything. She also felt sated in ways she never had before after what they'd just done. If she could live off his cock alone, the world would be a merry place.

Against his better judgment, Sebastian sat down opposite her and held out his hand. "Here."

"What?" Leona asked in confusion, lifting her head from its relaxed position. "No," she said, pushing his hand away from her.

"I don't mind. Maybe you won't like it. But I know you're curious," he said. "I'm not AB-negative, but... O-positive might be so common it's off-putting," he laughed.

Leona mulled this over, wondering if he was testing her. She couldn't find any sort of reason behind a trap other than that he'd just had a change of heart at the moment. "I'm not going to hurt you," she reassured, scooting to sit behind him. She wrapped her arms around his stomach, her palms flattening against his chest. Slowly, her tongue licked up his back to the puncture wounds from her nails through the rips on his shirt, the blood wiping clean in her path. Her pupils dilated and she gripped him tighter. Her fangs extended and she felt her control wavering, but she was aware of every move she made. She would *not* harm him.

Well, permanently.

Leona let her teeth sink into the nail-wounds and she began to drink. And drink. And drink.

"Leona," he breathed after a few moments, feeling only slightly clammy. "Leona."

She pulled back the second time he said her name. Her hands raked down his back, then she ran her thumb over the wounds she made. "Thank you. You are delectable. I feel closer to you now," she said. "I never think I can fall deeper in love with you and you prove me wrong every day. Every hour."

"I draw the line at every minute and second," he teased, turning around to face her. He took her face in his hands and kissed her. Their kiss was enough to make his toes curl. A metallic twang invaded their kiss, but it wasn't anything new. He often got wisps of it when she came home from feeding and woke him up with a kiss. She was *always* horny after a hunt, which was both a good and bad thing for him. Good in that he got sex that made him unable to sit directly on his ass for a week, but bad because he was unable to sit directly on his ass for a week.

"Hopefully Pookie's virgin ears didn't hear any of that," Leona said with a small giggle, causing Sebastian to chuckle. She pulled him by the neck for another kiss, and they collapsed to the floor to resume their last conversation.

22

"Let her have her fun, Gideon. You know she'll return to you when the moment is right."

Gideon eyed his oldest friend, Damien Hawthorne, and shook his head. "This charade has gone on long enough. At first, it was amusing, but now there's word that they've brought two new immortals into the fold. No doubt an attempt to shield her even more. What is her inane fascination with this human?"

They were at his castle in the North York countryside in England. It was made of grey stone, shrouded from the public by forest. Sometimes those exploring the national park nearby would wander too far and get lost, but they never made it back to their families. Gideon and his mates took care of them before they could cry out for help — not that anyone would have heard their screams in the first place.

There were streams of water near the castle, flowing evenly to feed the animals that hunted in the area. Shrubbery and flowers surrounded the front pathway, pebbles and gravel creating a trail down his estate.

Damien watched Gideon pace. He only ever saw him so worked up when Leona was involved. He usually couldn't be bothered with other issues and left them to himself or Theodore to sort out.

He had known Gideon for several centuries, having met him after the vampire tried to kill him. It had been a full moon, which amplified Damien's abilities, and he had nearly taken Gideon's head off. After an all-out bloodbath, and in fear for his life, Gideon drew a truce with the werewolf, and they worked together in tandem ever since. Damien was thankful for his friendship, because after he brought Leona into their world, and Whitney had been so happy to find a friend in her. His romance with her was one of intense passion and lust, which soon developed into love. When Leona escaped the first time and took the girls with her, he was angry and torn. He hadn't understood how Whitney could have left him, but when thinking about his loyalty to his friend, he started to come to terms with it. He did what he could to keep Gideon in the dark, but... he had been in his life much longer than Whitney had. Though she meant a great deal to him, she was only a woman in the end.

He had a much more complicated relationship with Theodore Selwyn, their other friend. Damien had turned him nearly 500 years ago in a complete accident. He had been intending to kill Theodore, but humans in Theodore's nearby village heard the commotion and came to investigate. Not wanting to be seen, Damien fled and found his dinner elsewhere. Theodore, however, was infected by his scratches, and left scarred for the rest of his life. He contracted lycanthropy, and on the next full moon, transformed completely. He had been a werewolf ever since.

Their conditions were different from the usual myths that humans spread. They did not only turn on the full moon, but their powers, such as strength, sight, and smell, were much more potent those nights. They could willfully turn at any moment, though it was much easier to hide in plain sight when they controlled their urges.

Theodore and Damien had come back together when Damien sensed a new wolf in his territory. Recognizing him, he took pity on him. Theodore did not take to his new identity well and had been terrorizing villages left and right. Damien urged secrecy, so he took him under his wing and began to train him. Over the next few years of their friendship, something stronger bloomed between them. Briefly — by their standards of time — they shared a clandestine affair, and had been wrapped up in each other for several decades.

But when Whitney came along, everything changed, and Theodore had been thrown to the wayside. Bitterness consumed him for a time as he watched his closest friend and lover do everything *they* used to do with someone else, but... that faded after a few years. He had grown close to Leona and Piper, and even Whitney eventually. He had been integral in Leona's escape, not that Gideon or Damien knew that. As far as they were concerned, Theodore had been traveling for a few days when everything went down. They hadn't cared about him enough to double-check his alibi. That had been the final straw for him, and his loyalty almost completely shifted to the girls.

When Damien wasn't feeling sorry for himself and wandering into his bedroom, that was.

Currently, Damien was lounging on a loveseat, his feet propped up on the arm. He was picking at a piece of wood with a whittling knife, creating a small fox. "If you're that bent out of shape about it, mate, just go *get her*. I'm tired of hearing you bitch and moan all the time about it. Are you scared of their new cronies?"

"No," Gideon scoffed, folding his arms. He hadn't fed in over a week and he was on edge. "Why does she keep running from me? Why is she so *unhappy*? Does she think I *want* to punish her? She must understand that she cannot behave that way. If she would just give in to how the world works, things would be much easier. She was never this combative when she was a human. She practically hung off every word that came from my mouth. It was one of the reasons I loved her so much," he muttered. "And now she deigns to sink so low as to lay with a *human*?" Gideon shook his head and made a gagging noise. "It's disgusting."

"I'm not getting in the middle of your feud with her. It almost got me killed last time. And Theo *still* hasn't forgiven me. Whitney is being pissy, too," he muttered. "You could have waited at least a few *days* before rocking up there to intimidate them. It made it so obvious that it was Whitney's doing. Now she's off with me."

"As if I give a shit as to what other people think or are concerned with. They needed to know to count their days. I need Leona to grow more attached to this *insect*, then when I squash him, perhaps she will truly be broken and capitulate to me. She needs to stop thinking there is some grandiose life for her outside of these walls. I am the most powerful immortal in the world… what more could she want?"

Damien stayed quiet and continued whittling. He knew better than to counter him when he was in a mood like this. "Don't ask me for help. You're on your own with this one, Gid," he mumbled.

The vampire shook his head, his red eyes dark with anger. "We'll see."

eona stared down at the corpse beneath her while wiping blood off her chin. Slowly, she nudged the man's body with her foot, turning him over. She had been *hungry*. It was the kind of craving that blood bags hadn't been able to quench, so she informed Sebastian she'd be going out for a quick hunt and to have a bath running for her when she got back. She smiled to herself at the thought of him; he was so kind and generous, and she never felt more loved than when in his presence.

It had been almost six months since Gideon had invaded Labasque Manor and threatened them. She was beginning to become more relaxed with the situation, drunk on love, and had started to go back and forth more between the girls' house and Sebastian's. It was fun training Charlotte and Victor, and Sebastian had even seemed to come to terms with everything. She had been worried for a while, unsure if it would be enough to break the trust they had in one another.

He had to understand that she had no part in that process, and she *understood* where he was coming from. Though, she was an advocate of having a choice. She could only warn them so much, but she would never take their autonomy away.

Leona grabbed the dead man's shirt and began lugging him toward a nearby canal. She loved hunting in New Orleans because there was *always* a body of water nearby leading into the Mississippi River, a neighboring swamp, or Lake Pontchartrain. Her kills weren't usually found where the scene of the crime happened, which gave her more immunity. Though, she didn't have any fingerprints or DNA that would link to anything human, so she never worried about it anyway. As *if* the police could arrest her and send her to jail. *Please.*

She had been hunting in the Lower Ninth Ward, which was eerily quiet for this time of night. The crime rate had spiked recently in the city, which she used to her advantage. Not that she advocated for people getting hurt, but a woman had to eat, after all.

As she was about to make her way back home, the thin hairs on the back of her neck stood up. She stopped in her tracks and felt so paralyzed with fear, she couldn't even turn around.

"Hello, flower."

Gideon.

Her eyes widened and she stayed in place, as if he wouldn't be able to see her or smell her if she remained motionless. A thousand thoughts flew threw her head, each more scared and hopeless than the last.

Gathering herself, she held her head high and turned

around. He was not going to detect weakness in her today. She would *not* run from him any longer. He would *not* put the fear of God into her *bones* anymore.

"Your protector isn't around. I'm surprised he doesn't tail you," Gideon laughed, stepping closer to her. He was dressed in one of his pristine black suits, as he usually was. There was a time when that had made Leona swoon, but now? She could hardly hold his gaze without feeling disgusted.

"He doesn't have to in order to know that I'm going back to his bed. He doesn't have to fear that I'm going to *run*," she snarled, glaring at him. "Not that I owe you *any* sort of explanation, Valdis."

"Valdis now, is it? That stings," he teased, tilting his head slightly to the side. "Why are you acting as if you are free? As if you are not *mine*? Your infatuation with this human is laughable, *pathetic*. And quite frankly, I've had enough of this party trick. It's time for you to come home."

"Infatuation?!" Leona laughed incredulously. "I'm in love with him. I'm *his*. I don't belong to you," she said, though it felt like swallowing nails. The venom in her body was reacting to her blatant dismissal of him. She knew he was flexing his powers against her, trying to make her bend so hard she broke. That would not happen. Though she was happiest when she was away from him, her body couldn't help but feel *betrayal*. She grounded herself and continued, "You have others. Why me? Why this obsession with *me*?"

Gideon answered by grabbing her throat and slamming her against a nearby wall, dust crumbling around them from the hit. He held her there while she struggled, her nails clawing at his arm and hand. "*You* belong to me, Leona. Don't you dare even *think* otherwise," he murmured darkly, his tone dripping with warning. Gideon slammed her head back against the wall, Leona crying out in pain. Her vision blurred for a moment, her body limp as he quickly whirled her around and shoved her face-first against the brick of the wall. His voice was hot by her ear, "I'll show you how I know you belong to me."

"Gideon, *stop*, you fucking bastard," Leona gasped desperately, tears streaming down her face. "Get off me!"

She screamed and pushed back with all her might, but to no avail. He hadn't even budged. She tried to use any of her powers against him, but her mind was clouded with the barrier their bond kept strong. Her body was almost actively going against her, responding in kind to the venom that was *longing* for its sire. She was hurting *herself*.

"I love *Sebastian*," she sobbed. "I love him so much." Gideon's hand found its way under the dress she was in, his knees keeping her legs spread just far enough apart. "Stop," she begged, willing for *anything* but this. Trying to push back at his hands, he responded with a tighter grip on her wrists; so tight that it *actually* caused her to wince in pain.

When she felt him enter her, her entire world came thundering down around her. She sobbed as he violently took her from behind, her brain sending distress signals, but the venom evaporated them before they could reach her muscles. She thrashed the entire time, trying anything to get him to let her go. Her face was harshly grinding into the rough brick of the wall, her teeth feeling like they were going to shatter with the pressure of his hold.

She was back in Hell. How cruel the world was to waste her immortality by binding her to a monster who had abused her for more than 300 years. It didn't seem like that trend was going to stop any time soon.

Was this all she was good for? To be his playtoy? To be the mat under his boot? She squeezed her eyes shut and thought of Sebastian, thought of the fact that he would probably never see her again. What would he think? Would he think that she just abandoned him? Would the girls tell him what happened when they inevitably found out? All she had wanted was happiness, a chance at a *normal* life — she felt like the naive little girl that had been so enthralled with Gideon the moment she laid eyes on him. She wished more than anything she could go back to that day when he'd waltzed into her father's estate, asking for her hand to dance. She hadn't recognized him, which had been a chunk of the appeal. A foreign lord asking for *her* hand? A lowly Abrin daughter? It was her dream come true.

Now, only nightmares festered between them.

Gideon fisted her hair and yanked her head back, her neck exposed and stretched out. He leaned down and harshly bit the skin, puncturing her jugular. He sucked hard, moaning into the crook of her neck. Drinking another vampire's blood was not the same as a human's. Much like a human being comprised of mostly water, though drinking regular water from a human body was impossible, the same was said for a vampire. Drinking another's blood merely strengthened the connection between them and gave them a glimpse into their feelings. Gideon had gotten so used to overpowering his prey, he hardly noticed the pain Leona was in. His pleasure was too paramount.

"I hate you," she whispered weakly, staring blearily up at the night sky. The stars shimmered, and she wished more than anything to be one of them. Nothing was worth this, no promise of eternal life or beauty — not even the love she felt for Sebastian. Because the pain of losing him would be her undoing.

Gideon drained her enough to weaken her. He didn't need her fighting and thrashing on their trip back to England. He came hard inside her, Leona whimpering in discomfort as he growled obscenities in her ear. Pulling out of her, he did his trousers back up with one hand, the other still keeping her in front of him. "Who do you belong to, Leona?"

"Sebastian."

Her cheek exploded in pain and her mind took several seconds to process his harsh punch. She crumpled against the wall, blood staining her dress.

"Who do you belong to?"

"Fuck you," she spat, blood spraying over his face.

He wiped it off, smearing it over his hand and pale cheeks and neck. His crimson eyes flicked to her, and he retorted with yet another punch, her bones cracking beneath the blow. "Who. Do. You. Belong. To?"

Leona was practically choking on her own blood, unable to answer. She shifted her eyes to his, hoping her glare from hell would answer his question. Gideon snarled in response, a low and terrifying groan resonating deep in his throat. He snatched her by the neck and hoisted her in the air. "I will *ensure* you gag on your insolence when this is over. I will chain you to the wall and make you watch as I skin your little boyfriend alive. I will have him begging for a God that *will not answer.* He will only see your face as he reaches his end. Or perhaps I'll turn him and have you watch his suffering for all eternity. He will look to you and *yearn* for the day before he met you. And you will only have yourself to blame when I finally put him out of his misery and dump his guts down your throat."

Her eyes were wide with terror, her entire body quaking. "Don't hurt him," she said quietly. "Please."

Gideon pulled her close to him, his breath so close it shifted her eyelashes. "You are in no position to bargain, flower."

"I won't ever leave again," she pleaded in a broken whisper. "I will remain yours forever. Just… don't touch him."

Gideon smirked and gently trailed his nose up her cheek, causing her to flinch violently. He held her in place, his tongue moving to caress the deep gashes that had formed along her jaw. "Is that so?" he purred. "Your word doesn't hold much weight anymore, my dear. How am I to trust you?"

"Do anything you want to me," she cried. "I'm *begging* you. Don't touch him. Take me back— back *home*, and forget all of this happened."

"Home?" he repeated, pulling back to look at her. "Where is your home, Leona?"

She looked at him, bile threatening to come up her throat. In defeat, her shoulders slumped, and she finally broke. "With you."

A wretched smile unfurled around Gideon's lips and he nodded. "Never forget that again."

24

Sebastian stared at the bath that had since run cold. Victor, Charlotte, Piper, and Whitney were pacing around his house, trying to figure out a plan of action. It had become blindingly obvious that she had been taken, and it didn't take him three guesses to figure out who was behind the kidnapping. Sebastian had briefly wondered if she was just taking her time with the hunt, but she had assured him she wouldn't be gone for longer than a few hours.

That was six hours ago.

Sebastian had called her friends, asking if they had seen her, but they hadn't. Panic started to set in and in just a few moments, the four vampires were practically beating down his door. Victor and Charlotte had kept him company, tried to keep him calm, while Piper and Whitney went out to try and track her. They had returned in less than an hour, explaining that they'd found traces of her blood, and had smelled Gideon's scent. It made him sick. Multiple times.

Now, he was just numb. Numb, but scared and angry. He knew that she hadn't gone willingly. There was no question in his mind about her loyalty to him, and Gideon was threatened by that. All he knew was to take her by force. That monster would never understand the concept of love or consent. Sebastian just *prayed* she wasn't hurt too badly.

"Sebastian, come in here," Charlotte said, by his side all of a sudden. Gently, she placed her hand on his shoulder, which made him jump. Her eyes softened and her frown deepened. "Please."

He obeyed and followed her into the living room where everyone else was. They all looked hopeless, like they were about to tell him his puppy died, and he hated it. Had they given up? Surely not?

"What are we going to do? When are we going to go get her?" Sebastian asked, breaking the silence.

"It's not that simple…" Piper started with a glance toward Whitney.

"Why isn't it?!" Sebastian snapped. "It actually *is* that simple. It's five against one. We will come up with a plan and we will beat him."

"Sebastian, maybe *we* should just go…"

"You honestly think I'm just going to sit on my ass while you go find her? You could use my help. If you're so damn scared of him, you need the backup. Where does he live? Somewhere here in the U.S.?"

"No," Whitney sighed, shaking her head. "He lives in an estate in the countryside in England. He'll see us coming from miles off. Not to mention Damien and Theodore are probably both there, and they'll smell us before even Gideon does. There will be no element of surprise."

"Aren't you fucking Damien?" Sebastian asked crudely. "Aren't *you* the reason Gideon knew where Leona was in the first place? You let slip to your boyfriend that she was here in New Orleans. Now look what happened."

"Sebastian, none of the blame lies with anyone in this room," Piper said warningly. "You are misplacing your anger. We *are* scared of Gideon because he is powerful and terrifying. You are underestimating him."

"I'm not—"

"*Yes*, you are. Don't talk about things you don't know shit about," Piper cursed with her brows furrowed. "We aren't just going to leave Leona to die, but we *do* need to come up with a plan. That plan is not going to include you. He will kill you instantly before any of us can even blink. He will ensure you feel pain. He *wants* to hurt Leona. That means hurting you beyond comprehension. He will punish her through you."

"Listen to me," Sebastian said darkly as he squared up to the blonde. "The only way you're going to keep me from coming with you is if you kill me. I know your kind can't feel pain, but he *will*. Leona will be freed of his shackles once and for all and she will never have to look over her shoulder again. If you don't take me with you or tell me where his *estate* is, I will find it myself."

"This is serious," Piper said in a last-ditch effort.

"No shit it's serious!" Sebastian hissed, throwing his hands up. "Anyone can be killed. There is no such thing as *true* immortality. He is not a god. You should stop fearing him like he is. Just because he's a billion years old, or however fucking long he's been around, does *not* mean he can't be beat. Nobody's ever had the balls to try is all," he said. "Whatever we need to do to get ready is what we're going to do. You turned Charlotte and Victor to help protect me, to fight him. Didn't you?" he asked, staring at all of them. "Well, now's the time. I'm *asking you* to fight for me. For Leona. For the family you claim I'm a part of. I'm willing to put my life down for all of you. Are you?"

Victor sighed after an age of silence, then turned to his fellow immortals. "Sebastian is right. We can't leave Leona out to dry. She's probably scared and hurt. Gideon will have an edge because we'd be bringing a fight to him, but at this point, it doesn't look like we have a choice. We need to stay strong. Like Bas said, there are five of us and one of him. And when Leona's freed, that'll be six to one. We can even ask Theodore to—"

"Theo and Dame won't fight him," Whitney interrupted, folding her arms. "They won't fight *with* him if we're involved — if *I'm* involved — but they won't go against him either."

"Fine," Sebastian interjected. "Just us then. He knows what to expect with you two," he said, eyeing Piper and Whitney. "But Charlie and Victor are new vampires. He doesn't have experience with them. And humans are more powerful than you think," he said.

"Sebby, a gun isn't going to work on him," Charlotte said, knowing where this was going.

"I'm going to try anyway," he mumbled. "It'll at least distract him long enough for one of you to go after him and try and knock him down."

"Sebastian can hold his own," Victor said, not wanting anyone else to dismiss him. It was pointless. "I've seen him in a fight. I know it's a human against a vampire, but he won't run and hide. He always finds his way out," he smirked, draping his arm over his shoulder.

Sebastian nodded and looked at the other three. "It's settled then. Let's go fuck him up."

25

eona sat and stared at the specks of dust littering the stone walls of her dungeon. She didn't know how long she'd been there. She was hungry, weak, and broken.

Mostly, she was furious.

Rage filled her more than it ever had before, but she was too physically weak to fight back or do much about it. Yet again, this monster was trying to keep her in his prison. She wasn't shackled to the wall, which surprised her. He must have had some sort of pity on her after she'd passed out following his assault back in Louisiana. Looking down at her grimy hands, she clenched them together so hard, her nails punctured the skin of her palm and made her bleed. The liquid was a deep red, darker than she'd ever seen come from herself before. She chalked it up to her hunger. Her eyes were probably a deeper green than usual, too — not that she'd be brave enough to catch a glimpse of her reflection anywhere.

More than likely, she wouldn't even recognize herself.

Once upon a time, his castle had been so full of light. Not physically, of course, but the way it was decorated, the way it felt when she walked around, the way she imagined her *future* being here with him forevermore. Her parents had even come to visit once, while she was still human. Little did any of them know, Gideon had murdered his own parents and ripped their heritage from them *eons* before. Her parents had approved of him, as they always would have, as *he* always intended. She had been so smitten, so in love, and hadn't seen any of the warning signs. He was far too good to be true, and in hindsight, she wished she would have listened to the warning bells sounding off in her young, naive head. She wouldn't know Sebastian now, of course, but she also wouldn't be putting them both through this pain.

She thought about him and wondered what he was doing. What did he think happened? Did he think she left him for Gideon? In her bones, she knew that wasn't true, but the poisonous demons whispering in her ears were trying to convince her otherwise. Logically, she knew he would have gone to their friends, and Whitney and Piper would know where she'd been taken. More than anything, she prayed they kept Sebastian safe and *far away* from this place.

But knowing that man — that sweet, generous, kind man — he wouldn't sit idly so easily.

Leona screamed out in agony and frustration, slamming her fists back against the wall behind her so hard, dust rained down above her. Stone cracked against her hands and her body trembled with the effort. The last thing she wanted to do was cry, but it was becoming increasingly difficult not to. She didn't want to seem weak. She was *not* weak. She just didn't know why *she* of all people had been destined to this life of hell. In her mortal years, she had behaved as she should have: she was a virgin when she met Gideon, she had never kissed another person before him, she obeyed her parents, she wore respectable clothing, she did the chores asked of her. She thought she had done everything *right* and that Gideon was her reward of eternal happiness.

And look where that reward got her. A prison cell.

Briefly, it crossed her mind to just give in. If she gave in, her friends wouldn't have to risk themselves, and Sebastian would be free to move on and find someone who wouldn't hurt him this way — who wouldn't potentially drive him into a suicide mission.

Her thoughts were interrupted when a lock clicked and the steel door trapping her in creaked open. In walked Gideon, looking too smug for her liking. She wanted nothing more than to claw his fucking eyes and throat out.

"You've looked better," he said with a smirk, leaning against the wall near her with his hands in his trouser pockets.

"Go to hell," she spat, pushing herself to stand. "They'll be here. They'll—"

"Oh, will they? Where are they then, Leona?" Gideon said whilst raising his eyebrows, a look of pure amusement on his face. He glanced around, then looked up to the ceiling, then the floor. "Are they hiding in the cellar? The back garden? Behind one of the statues? They're doing a pretty shit job of rescuing you if so."

"They have gotten me back every time before. They'll do it again. You can't keep me. You don't *own* me. How many times do I have to prove that to you? And Sebastian, he'll—"

"He'll *what*, little flower? Throw some punches? *Photograph* me to death?" He scoffed. "You never learn, do you? How many times must *I* teach you this lesson by bringing you back? One day, you'll learn. Your friends are not a threat to me. Your *boyfriend* isn't."

"He should be."

At this, he barked a laugh. "Pardon me," he said dismissively, putting a hand on his chest. "How silly of me. You're *right*, Leona. I'm positively *quaking* in my boots about your human sex toy." He closed in on her, causing the woman to back up against the wall. Slowly, Gideon trailed his finger down her cheek. "Where are you standing right now, sweetheart? Who have you been loyal to since your conception?" he smirked, forcing her gaze to stay on him. He could sense her internal struggle. "Me. Enough with this Sebastian shit. That's done. You're staying here. You *will not* leave my side again. I have been patient with your childish games, but my patience has run out. You have broken my trust and my heart far too many times," he added. Leona snorted derisively, and Gideon harshly grabbed her cheeks with one hand, his long nails digging into her porcelain skin. "How am I to ever trust you with an *ounce* of freedom again? You'll be a caged bird for the next hundred years, and even then…"

As he trailed off, Leona forced a smile through his grip on her face. She laughed quietly, which caused Gideon to pull back in confusion. She just couldn't help herself. He was *delusional.* "You honestly believe that I could *ever* see you as anything other than a beast? One day I will rip you ear from ear. I will *end* you, Gideon. I will be the last thing you see before the light leaves your eyes and you're banished to your own personal circle of hell. You can keep me here in your pit all you want, but you will not own me. You will not *break* me ever again. I have experienced love, friendship, *true* loyalty. I have felt happiness that fills my body in such a way, I'm overwhelmed. I have felt all the things I longed to have since I was a girl. Sebastian has given me—"

Crack!

Leona's head smashed back against the stone wall, and she slowly slid down, her vision nearly blacked out. Blearily, she blinked up at Gideon. He had always moved much faster than her, which made him so difficult to fight. That, and her body had always willed her to pull her punches against him. The metallic twang of blood filled her nostrils and her glands salivated at the release.

"Your friends aren't coming for you. And if they do... I will ensure they — and you — regret it."

Leona opened her eyes slowly, having passed out from Gideon's earlier assault. She looked down at her tattered dress, noting stains that hadn't been there before. Judging by the ache between her legs, she assumed that monster had raped her again. She couldn't even *remember.* She felt somewhat helpless, being as physically weak as she was. With the rest of her remaining strength, she was *trying* not to be mentally weak. She was trying to stay strong, to have faith and hope; her friends had come for her all the other times, and they'd come for her now. No matter how long it took.

Though, the thought scared her. It scared her because she didn't bloody know what they were going to be walking into. Gideon was right, his patience had run out, and she doubted he'd let her go so easily this time. Perhaps he stopped having fun with this game they'd been playing for the last few centuries. Maybe she truly hadn't even seen the *real* him yet.

That terrified her.

Her eyes roamed to a rat that scurried across the ground. She was too weak to even reach out to grab it, let alone pounce on it and feed from it.

It was the first time in a long time that she was mildly convinced she'd actually die. It wasn't the worst thought in the world, given any circle of Hell would be better than this place, but... her thoughts always roamed back to Sebastian. She knew it was selfish and she *knew* she ought to let him go, but she couldn't.

She just prayed that if her friends came after her again, that somehow, some way, they convinced him to stay home. But as she thought already before... she knew deep down he wouldn't let them go without him.

She was pulled from her reverie at the sound of the door opening again. Her stomach flipped in reaction and instinctively, she plastered herself back against the wall where she sat. Gideon's tall, imposing form came into view, but he was carrying something with him. Papers? Pictures?

"Figured I could give you a little history lesson as we wait," Gideon cooed, leaning down to toss the papers on her lap. "Recognize any of those texts, darling?"

Leona looked down and skimmed over the words, her vision slightly blurry. Blinking a few times to rid herself of the grogginess, she focused. "A vampire hunter? So what?"

"You don't recognize him at all?"

Leona focused on the picture, then flicked her eyes up at Gideon. "This is the one you made me go after when I was first turned. Because he was targeting you and nearly got you," she said.

"I wouldn't say *nearly*, but yes. Recognize anything else? How about that surname?"

Leona was tired of the back-and-forth with him. Why did he always have to test her about everything? It was his condescending nature that made her bloody skin crawl. She looked down at the words by the picture, then furrowed her brows. Her eyes quickly cut to the picture, and she held it closer to her. Blinking a few more times, she wanted to make sure she was actually seeing what she thought…

"Ah, now you're with us. Bravo," Gideon said sarcastically. "I always knew you were a masochist, but I didn't know it was to *this* extent. Fucking a vampire hunter. Or at least… a watered-down version."

"Just because this bloke looks like Sebastian and has a similar surname doesn't mean they're related," Leona said as she tossed the documents down on the ground. "What is the point of all this?"

"Well, I wanted to do some homework on your *toy* is all.

Imagine my surprise when I come across this juicy detail. You know, when I saw him, I thought I knew him from somewhere. I just couldn't place it. I wouldn't say he's his double, but... the comparison between your beloved Sebastian and our *darling* Xavier is rather hard to ignore, don't you think?"

"He's not a vampire hunter. He's a regular man. Is that what this is about? Wiping out the lineage?"

"I thought we already did that, but it appears that insect got busy between murdering my friends," Gideon sighed, leaning down to pick up the papers. "It's not wholly about him — most of it's about punishing you — but now I'll take even more pleasure in killing him when I see him again. I'd rather save that for the grand finale though. Make sure everyone is there to see it. You especially."

Leona bit back her curse, knowing it would only land her in hot water. She could barely even keep her head up and her eyes open, she didn't need to be bashed against the wall again.

"How could you not have noticed while you were fucking him?"

Leona did scoff at that. "I never fucked Xavier. I wasn't exactly thinking of the people we've killed in the past while I was in bed with Sebastian."

Though, all of this made sense. It explained the pull she had toward him right at the beginning, right at that first sight. She had thought it was true love, but now she felt silly. It was because her natural instincts were screaming at her to either go to him and take him out, or run as far away as she could from him.

Gideon had been saving face. Xavier *had* been close to

killing him. At least as close as anyone else had ever gotten. She couldn't believe she'd forgotten about that. It had been so long ago, and she hadn't known any better. She hadn't known the true danger they'd been in; but thinking back on it now, how feral and panicked Gideon had been... No wonder he was so bent out of shape about Sebastian now. It *did* go deeper than his possession over Leona.

"I'll take great pleasure in ending his short, miserable life. I'll take even greater pleasure ensuring you watch every second of it," Gideon said. "How does that make you feel?"

Leona didn't respond. Any response had the potential to piss him off, and she needed *no* help doing that at the moment. Gideon, seemingly disappointed by her not taking the bait, left the room and let her be. The redhead sagged in relief and closed her eyes.

All she could hope for was a miracle at this point.

26

Sebastian knelt at the base of his small closet in his bedroom, rifling through a few things on the floor. He pushed aside shoes and some clothes that had fallen off their hangers and finally found what he'd been looking for.

He pulled out a small, locked, dark box. Leaning back on his heels, he stared at it for nearly a minute. His breathing became slightly labored and it was as if time stood still. He reached into his pocket for his house keys and shifted to a very small one hidden on the ring. While he inserted it into the box's lock, the tremor in his hand grew more dramatic. Turning the key, a small *click!* sounded and he took the key out.

Opening the box revealed a small cloth. Sebastian unraveled it and stared down at the black Magnum handgun lying there. It looked so... normal, despite it being the chain holding the wrecking ball that shattered his life so many years ago. Gently, carefully, as if it would burn him if he made the wrong move, he ran his fingers over the cool metal. Images raced through his mind of the horrible night he lost his poor mother. All the screams, the shouts, the bangs, the metallic scent piercing through the air so much that he had nearly forgotten how to breathe, all came flooding back to his senses.

After he shot his father, Victor had been the first one he called. He had been so distraught on the phone that the blonde hadn't even known what happened until he got there and saw the scene. The next call was to Mr. Labasque, who was over just as quick. If Sebastian didn't know better, he'd have thought this wasn't the first murder Victor's dad had seen before. Everything had moved so quickly — too quickly. Sebastian lost parts of that day forever, his brain blocking them from ever being retrieved. Victor's father had instructed his son to get the murder weapon and get rid of it. It wasn't until years later that Sebastian found it hidden away in Victor's basement along with some Christmas decorations. He had never mentioned it to his friend, considering it was a piece of evidence, and bringing up that day was never a good idea. But he supposed hiding it with pretty lights and garland was as good a place as any. He would have gone with the bottom of the bayou, but... it wasn't his call. And they had been little more than teenagers.

But now, he was thankful. Because every wrong that gun helped commit was about to be reversed when he buried as many bullets as he could into the devil himself.

Sebastian was pulled from his reverie by knocking on the door. He grabbed the gun and closed the box. Hiding it again, he put the gun in the pocket of his coat and stood up to go to the front of the house.

Opening the door, Sebastian met eyes with too many fucking immortals. How had his life come to this?

"You ready to go?" Whitney asked. "You got your wooden stakes and garlic knots?"

"And silver bullets to match," Sebastian sighed. They had instructed him to pack light — he couldn't even bring a bag with him. But the thought of being in the same clothes for however long wasn't really the priority in his head. He'd go nude if it meant getting Leona back safely.

The dark-haired man stepped out of the threshold of the front door and locked the place up. "Let's get the hell out of here."

Though Sebastian had evanesced with Leona short distances throughout the city, they had never had the chance or reason to travel further than that. Doing so across an entire ocean made his head spin. Piper had carried him and Charlotte, and Whitney had carried Victor. Though Charlotte had shown great potential with evanescing as a new vampire, Piper and Whitney stressed that they would need their entire strengths to go against Gideon, and they couldn't risk Charlotte or Victor tiring themselves out beforehand with the travel. Plus, this journey was one the older vampires had made countless times.

Not necessarily with two new vampires and a human in

tow, but… first time for everything.

Sebastian had been sick practically the entire time, his nerves consuming him. His brain was whirring with constant worries about Leona. Was she okay? Was she hurt? Was she *alive*? Was she even at this psychopath's castle? Both Whitney and Piper assured him this was a pattern, and this would be the most likely place she'd be. Gideon was far too arrogant to stay hidden from his home. But they had taken her multiple times before, they could do it again.

Whitney had not been able to get much information from Damien on the situation. She had briefly been in contact with him via phone when they landed in England, but that was it. He had hurriedly told her to go back home and not start this again, but she was having none of it. She knew he wouldn't be there to fight against them, but he wouldn't be there to fight *with* them either. She had also heard nothing from Theodore, which meant he was likely with Damien during their conversation and had heard everything. Usually, he was the most level-headed of the group, and stayed in the neutral zone. But… a fight with Gideon wasn't something *anyone* wanted to be caught in the middle of.

The closest they were able to evanesce to Gideon's estate was the outskirts of the woods surrounding the property. He would be able to sense and smell their magic otherwise, and the element of surprise was *everything* to their mission. All Sebastian could do was take in the scenery as they went on their hike through the forest. It was the only distraction his brain could latch onto in the moment.

He just prayed they weren't too late. He hoped her spirits

weren't broken and that she knew in her heart they would rescue her.

He was also grappling with the fact that he was probably about to die. Closing his eyes, it took everything to keep his breathing calm. His friends were concerned, but they knew better than to bother him at the moment. They had tried, all the way up until they started their trek to the forest, to talk him out of coming. They'd probably try some more on their hike and before they eventually made their way into Gideon's castle. Nothing they could say would ever change his mind.

He had been at peace with the thought of dying for years now — decades, even. Not that he ever thought his demise would come from a jealous, controlling vampiric overlord, but there were *less* cool ways to die, he supposed. Overall, he would be giving his life so she could get away, she could escape and be happy. Maybe with all of them combined, Gideon would finally be defeated and nobody would have to look over their shoulders anymore. If *that* was possible, then… he'd happily lay his life down for their futures.

The hike wasn't as long as he predicted, given Victor had picked Sebastian up to speed things along. He hadn't minded. Whatever got them there the quickest was what he wanted to do.

They hid behind a thick wall of trees, glimpses of Gideon's castle poking through the foliage. Sebastian stared up at it, his heart racing. She was in there. He knew it.

And he was going to get her out.

"There's a servants' entrance around the back," Whitney said quietly, looking between them. "I'm unsure if he's closed it off. We used it last time. If he hasn't, it will lead us into the slave quarters, which is near the dungeon. Leona *might* be there. Unless he's decided to keep her elsewhere. Best case scenario, we grab her before Gideon even knows we're there, and we get the fuck out of there *hopefully* with all our heads attached to our bodies."

"And... the worst case?" Charlotte asked, her eyebrows stitched together in concern.

"He finds us and kills all of us," Piper deadpanned, folding her arms. "But thinking about that possibility isn't going to do anyone any good. We need to focus. We need to be quiet. Sebastian's scent is a problem. It will be a miracle if he hasn't caught it already. He can't move as fast or quiet as us. He's a liability."

"No offense taken," Sebastian muttered with a roll of his eyes. "I know I'm not as badass as everyone here, but I have a weapon, I'm used to fighting, and I am quicker than most on my feet. I used to break into houses for money growing up. I know how to sneak around."

"One of you needs to stay with Sebastian at all times. It might be enough to mask his scent," Piper added, looking between everyone. "We're going to go in and pray we can get to the dungeons without being seen. Then, we're going to pray some more that Leona is actually there. If she *isn't*, we'll need to split up and go looking for her. Whitney and I will be able to catch her scent, so we'll go in pairs. Well... one trio," she said, glancing at Sebastian. "But we need to accept that Gideon will probably find us before we find her. We need to distract him long enough to get to her, then just try to make a run for it. Fighting him is useless."

"You know he's going to try to fight," Whitney said. "There's four of us now. Not two."

"Five," Sebastian cut in.

"Four *immortals*," Whitney corrected. "And a gun. At the very least, a gunshot will catch him off guard and distract him momentarily. All we need is a *moment*."

Piper looked at her dubiously, then sighed. "A moment is the best chance we have."

27

Leona was surrounded by drained rat carcasses. It was all she had to survive. She was lucky Gideon had even allowed her that much. Her head had healed from his last violent attack, but her heart and spirit weren't so quick to bounce back. She had told herself — and Gideon — that she would not lose hope, but... it was difficult. Ever since she'd entered into this immortal contract with her master, she formed a habit of fearing the worst. Because the worst was all that happened most of the time.

Taking a deep breath, she inhaled, trying to calm herself down. Then... she froze. Her eyes flew open and she inhaled again, catching a whiff of...

Sebastian.

Both fear and elation crippled her. She knew he was here, somewhere, and *prayed* it wasn't Gideon who brought him in. Inhaling again, she caught the scent of Whitney, Piper... They were here, just like they always were. She turned her head toward the door and scrambled to her feet. If this was anything like last time, she needed to be ready to go. The first time, Gideon hadn't locked her away, and it had been rather easy to slip out. After that, he learned from his mistake and imprisoned her when he wasn't around. This time... no matter if he was there or not, she was bound.

She pressed her ear against the door, trying to listen for *anything*. She could smell Gideon near too, and her body felt colder than usual with the terror flowing through her. As she heard footsteps, she backed off, her face hopeful. As the door burst open, her eyes fell on...

"You fucking whore," Gideon hissed, his eyes red and bright with fury. "I *know* your little friends are hiding around here somewhere. Are they in here?"

"No," Leona said, trying to keep her voice even. "But they'll find me eventually. I told you, you will *lose*. They're here. My *saviors* are here to rescue me. Again. How many times do we have to go through this before you realize it's pointless, Gideon? *That* is what loyalty is."

Gideon grabbed her by the throat and tried to force her mouth open, a small vial in his hand with an amber, murky liquid sloshing around inside. She screamed and curled her fingers around his hands, barely keeping him off her. Eventually, she managed to get her hand on the glassware and crushed it, the contents pouring out on both their hands. When he pulled back, she took her chance and bolted out of the room. A rush of adrenaline pumped through her, despite her hunger, and the thought of seeing Sebastian and escaping was the main thing spurring her on.

As she rounded a corner, she was suddenly grabbed. She thrashed against the person, until a familiar voice brought her out of her fearful trance.

"Leona!" Piper gasped, gripping her as tight as she could so she didn't run away. "Where is Gideon?! We were going to come to find you, but we heard him come and broke apart so he didn't find us. We needed to throw him off Sebastian's scent."

"Where is Sebastian?!" Leona practically shrieked in fear. "He's down there and he's *pissed*. We have to find Sebastian and get him the hell out of here before Gideon—"

"Before Gideon what?" a dark voice said from the other side of the room. Leona and Piper both turned to look at him, and Leona's eyes widened. Gideon stood, Sebastian on his knees beside him, struggling under the grip the vampire had on his head and hair. "Aww..." Gideon tutted, poking out his lower lip. "Didn't quite go to plan, did it? He was much easier to chase after than you, flower. And I met your new friends," he said, glancing toward Victor, Charlotte, and Whitney. "I would say the backup was a good call, but... bringing a snack along the way probably wasn't the strategy I would have gone with."

"Let him go," Leona said shakily. She tried to step toward him, but Piper kept her pulled back. "Let him go. Now, Gideon."

"Why in the hell would I want to do that? He only just got here, Le, I want to give him a grand tour. Bloke didn't even have the decency to knock on the front door," he pouted, before dragging him across the room. Sebastian grunted in pain and brought his hands up to claw at Gideon's vice above him. Gideon walked through to the open foyer, then tossed Sebastian in front of him like he weighed nothing more than a doll. Sebastian tumbled and braced himself on his hands and knees, his head screaming from the pain.

"Ah, ah," Gideon said, putting his hand out as Leona, Whitney, Piper, Charlotte, and Victor quickly followed behind him. He glanced over his shoulder, then turned so he could face all six of them. "He stays over there. You stay over there. That's how the rules work," he said, pointing to either side of the room. "I want you all to have a good seat to watch our brave, *darling* Sebastian's final act."

"I'm not afraid of you," Sebastian said, causing Gideon's attention to whip to him.

"You really are stupid," Gideon laughed, turning his body completely toward Sebastian. Leisurely, he strolled over to him, his fingertips arched together. "Why are you so hellbent on protecting her? You know you're nothing to her, don't you? Nothing but a momentary *distraction*. She tells me you don't want to be turned. If you were smarter, you'd abandon them and be here with me. Let me *teach* you about this life. Not the sentimental ways of women," he said, sneering at Leona, Whitney, Piper, and Charlotte. "I see they've already corrupted this one," he said, nodding to Victor. "You sure? It's not too late to choose the right side, Beliveau."

"You're fucking insane," Sebastian bit back.

"Pity. It's a shame, really. I'd like to see what someone like you could do as an immortal. However, your courage is conflated with idiocy. You're too annoying to be kept alive,"

Gideon said.

"I don't need to be an immortal to kill you," Sebastian spat. "Anything can be killed. You just have to know how to do it."

Gideon threw his head back and a laugh bellowed from him. "Is that so? Please, enlighten me. How *do* you kill me?"

"Rip you apart. Burn you. Poison you. Maybe some other things. Let's test my theories," Sebastian countered, reaching behind him. He pulled out his gun and aimed it toward him. "What about a half dozen bullets to the head?"

Gideon raised his eyebrows. "Color me impressed, human. This is a first, I'll admit. It looks like a nice firearm. You're confident in using it?"

"Confident enough to fuck your creepy face up," he growled, cocking the gun and moving his finger back over the trigger.

"Do it then," Gideon said. He smirked and tilted his chin up arrogantly, holding his arms out. "Will you quit stalling after this performance is over? Leona isn't exactly going to leave willingly without you."

Piper's eyes widened and she gripped Leona's hand. The plan had been to have Sebastian distract Gideon while she got Leona out, and the others were responsible for getting Sebastian out in the commotion of it all. As much as she knew Leona loved Sebastian, she was there for *her*, not him. If he died, well... Leona would get over it eventually. Whitney was safe because of Damien. Gideon hadn't killed her yet and she highly doubted he'd start today. And she could adequately protect Victor and Charlotte. Piper, however, hadn't accounted for the long list of supernatural abilities Gideon possessed and the link they all shared. She felt a fool.

"Go!" Sebastian yelled, knowing their plan was compromised. He squeezed the trigger as many times as he could, the gun echoing loudly throughout the room.

Six bullets pelted Gideon and he barely did so much as sway back. Two hit side-by-side on his forehead, another above his mouth, two on either side of his neck, and the last above his sternum. Some blood came out due to the impact, but Gideon didn't look much more bothered than if a mosquito had landed on him.

"Bravo," Gideon said, plucking the crushed casing of bullets out of his skin. His body began to morph back into his pristine state. He wiped the blood from him and licked it clean. "I'm sick of playing these games with you," he said, turning to look at the rest of them, who were bolted to the ground by the force of his gaze. "All of you die *tonight*. And Leona will live with it for the rest of her miserable existence."

Sebastian was hurriedly reloading the gun. He knew it was pointless, but he wasn't going to stand there and do nothing. Short of running at him and trying to tackle him or throw a punch, he was out of options.

Just as he was about to fire more rounds, Gideon lunged for Victor and Charlotte first. The blondes struggled against his grip, screaming and cursing to get him off. Piper, Leona, and Whitney were working together to pry him off their friends. Gideon reared his hand back and bat Whitney off him, letting go of Victor in the process. He still had Charlotte held tight in one hand. Leona and Piper managed to hold on and continued tearing away whatever they could of Gideon. Whitney rushed back toward him and bit his ear, ripping it off in a gush of blood. Gideon roared in pain and jerked his head back, bashing Whitney in the forehead. Once she was off him, Gideon's left hand joined his right in clamping around Charlotte's throat. It was a struggle with Leona and Piper still hanging off him. The grip made Charlotte cough violently, then she raked her nails down his hands, failing to loosen his grip.

Sebastian was by Victor and Whitney's sides, checking to see if they were okay. They seemed dazed from Gideon's strength, but otherwise unharmed... for the most part.

"Sebastian, go hide. Go far away from here. Leave the castle and hike back, go find civilization and *get yourself home*," Whitney panted.

"I'm not *leaving*!" Sebastian snapped. He was angry with the lack of confidence in him. He didn't have their powers, but he would *not* abandon them in any circumstances. He looked around and tried to find *anything* that would help. The room was decorated with things he'd only seen in movies or history books. Suits of armor, ancient artwork, and sculptures. He spotted some thick cable wrapped around some of the pillars of art Gideon had. As Victor and Whitney went back to help Charlotte, Sebastian ran to the pillar and began prying the steel cable off. Soon, he had a long piece in his hands, and he darted back to the group. Launching himself, he hooked the cable around the front of Gideon's neck and yanked back with all the force he could muster. It was enough to catch the vampire off guard, and his grip faltered from Charlotte.

She coughed violently, her neck purple and her eyes red with blood. She rolled over and gasped, trying to get her vision back in check.

Sebastian's attack didn't do anything except piss Gideon off more. He threw Sebastian off him and he hit the stairs in the middle of the room, the marble cracking under the force of his body. He cried out in pain and tried to push himself up, but he knew several things were broken.

"ENOUGH!" Gideon boomed, the shockwave of anger sending everyone else flailing back. As they recovered, he stormed over to Sebastian and picked him up by the throat. Sebastian groaned in agony and mauled at the monster's wrists to try to get some airflow. Gideon slowly lifted him up, his feet dangling off the ground.

"Sebastian!" Leona wailed, trying to get to him, but she was being held back.

Gideon smirked and looked over at all of them, then directly at Leona. "*This* is what you left me for? How pitiful," he cooed, turning his attention back to Sebastian. "Look at him. Quivering in fear."

Sebastian struggled to speak, his teeth gritted in pain. Kicking his legs, he tried to get some leverage. It was obvious to him now that Gideon liked to play with his food and make his prey suffer. Why else had he not just ripped Charlotte to shreds earlier? Why this *now*?

"Trying to beg for your life?" Gideon taunted, his head tilted ever so slightly.

"Never… begged before… not starting… now," Sebastian ground out, his vision fading in and out from the lack of oxygen.

"Aww…" Gideon sighed, pursing his lips. "Any last words?"

"Touch her again… and I'll… *kill you*," Sebastian managed, his voice barely above a strained whisper.

"Noted," Gideon laughed.

Then he shoved his hand into Sebastian's chest. The man's eyes widened in both shock and pain, and he coughed up blood, splattering it on Gideon's face. Gideon's hand went deeper into his body, then he dropped him, his hand coming out covered in crimson fluid. Lifting it up, his tongue glided over his fingers. "I can see why she kept you around. You are delicious," he sighed.

Sebastian was convulsing, gasping for any air he could. Blood poured from both his chest and mouth, and his vision was so blurry, he couldn't differentiate up from down.

Leona screamed, a gut-wrenching, wounded sound leaving her body. "No," she sobbed, nearly falling to the floor. She *just* about held herself up. Staggering to Sebastian, she dropped to her knees, knowing what she had to do. She had minutes — maybe not even that. "I'm sorry, darling," she cried, tears falling on him. He was so pale. His eyes didn't even look like his anymore. "I'm sorry. I have to. I *have* to."

Her fangs extended and she started to lean down, but hesitated. She couldn't let him die, but… was this doing what she had promised him wouldn't happen? She was taking his choice away. She hadn't asked to be turned. She hadn't been given a chance to choose. He had told her multiple times, no matter what, that he didn't want this life.

It felt like searing pain was shooting through her as each millisecond passed. Almost like she'd been stabbed. It was different than any sort of fear or heartbreak she had ever endured. This went deeper than her *bones*.

Victor, Piper, and Whitney were holding Gideon back from coming any closer to the couple. Fueled with rage, all three of them almost matched Gideon's power, and he was struggling. It was buying them time. As much as they could get.

Leona's hands shook and she knew she had no choice. She... She didn't. Did she? He was *dying*.

But she couldn't.

Staring down at him, wide-eyed and full of fear, she watched him take what had to be his last few attempts at breaths—

The next moment, Charlotte shoved her aside and sunk her teeth into his neck. She ripped into his throat, letting her venom seep from her fangs and into his jugular. She pulled back and bit again on the other side, and repeated the process for both wrists and both thighs.

All Leona felt was horror. The man she loved — if he wasn't too far gone — would despise her for the rest of time for catapulting him into an existence he never wanted. One that he *actively* refuted. And for what? For *her*? Was she worth such a thing? Was she worth *this*?

For a moment, she wondered if dying the most excruciating death, and even *losing* him, would be better than an eternity of him hating her.

"Leona," Charlotte said. When she got no answer, she

used a hand to wrench her face toward her, blood smearing on her cheeks. "Leona, look at me. You have to get it together. We *have* to go now."

"But— Sebastian, he—"

"He will be fine. But that's *only* if we leave. They can't hold Gideon off much longer, and I'm not strong enough to evanesce back home with both of you in my arms. The others will follow behind us."

"Gideon will come after us—"

"We will go where they can't find us. I promise you. Victor and I have worked out a plan. But you have to trust us. Okay? Have you been to New York City before?"

"Yes," Leona said, not understanding how this was relevant.

"Okay," Charlotte said with a nod. "Take us there. If you can get us somewhere discreet where we won't be around a bunch of people — an alley, *something* — then I can get us the rest of the way back to my place. We'll be safe and he won't know where we are. At least until we can get Sebastian cleaned up and recovered. All we're doing is buying time."

"Okay," Leona stammered. "Okay, okay," she repeated, trying to get her thoughts together. She gathered Charlotte and a bloodied and unconscious Sebastian in her arms, and with Gideon's attention elsewhere, evanesced them out of the country.

28

Leona collapsed in a heap with Charlotte and Sebastian, who was still lifeless. They had arrived in a darkened and — *thankfully* — abandoned alleyway. The hum of nightlife was evident in their surroundings, and the faint hue of streetlights and billboards was visible in the distance.

"We made it," Charlotte breathed, looking over Sebastian. She had never actually seen the process take place. Victor and she had been turned at the same time, so she had been preoccupied with her own change to catalogue what her husband had gone through. But… venom was an interesting thing, as Piper had once explained to her, and she just had to trust they hadn't been too late. It was the best chance they had.

Leona rested back against the grimy wall, unable to look at Sebastian. If he was dead… she couldn't bear it. Plus, her vision was going in and out and she was on the verge of passing out. Not only had she not fed properly in too long, she had used the rest of her minimal energy to get them here. She was overexerted, and wasn't even sure if she could walk.

Charlotte got up and quickly went to the edge of the street, glancing around to get her bearings. In a flash, she was back by their sides. "We aren't far from my place. Come on. Can you stand?"

"No," Leona said, her eyes closed. "I can't... do anything," she added breathily, her chest heaving.

"Alright," she said. Gathering the woman in her arms, she hoisted her over her shoulder, and did the same with Sebastian. Speed was her friend in that situation, and they made it a few dozen blocks throughout the heart of the city to the apartment she owned in the Upper East Side.

It took some doing to get them through the door without any passersby noticing them, but eventually, she got them both inside. Leona sat on the floor as Sebastian laid on Charlotte's living room sofa, his eyes closed. She stared at him, Charlotte having disappeared to get the bath going so they could help clean him up.

The redhead's thoughts were everywhere at once. The venom affected everyone differently. For her, the change had happened in a few minutes. Apparently, for Victor, it had been hours. For Charlotte, days. She traced her fingers gently down his cheek, which was paler than usual. She couldn't smell life on him anymore, but she couldn't sense or smell the decaying process either. Perhaps it was wishful thinking, but she wanted to believe Charlotte had gotten to him in time.

Guilt flooded her wholly. She had been too scared, too

paralyzed with anxiety, to change him and save his life. Charlotte had swooped in to rescue him. Would he hate her too? Would he turn against his dearest friends completely due to a chaotic, spur-of-the-moment decision to save him? She knew nobody in the world respected him and his standpoint more than the Labasques, but... at what selfish cost did they preserve his life? Now he was doomed to an existence he despised.

"Okay, come on," Charlotte said as she grabbed Sebastian and carefully lifted him up. "Help me get him undressed and into the bath. He won't want to be covered in blood when he wakes up."

"What if he doesn't wake up?" Leona asked nervously.

Just then, before Leona could even blink, a hard slap came across her cheek. She stared at Charlotte in shock. It hadn't hurt, just surprised her.

"Get your shit together," Charlotte hissed. "He is *going* to wake up. He's fine. His body is already starting to heal," she said, gesturing to the wound in his chest that wasn't *so* gory anymore. She then pointed to his neck, which was slowly stitching itself back together. Slowly. "We have no choice but to hope everything is fine. We left the love of my life and *your* two best friends at that psycho's place. We *have* to hope that they will make it back here okay and we will have time to get a game plan together. But right now, worrying about it or pitying ourselves isn't going to help. Do you understand me?"

Leona nodded, her chest tight with indignation. She huffed a breath, squashed her exhaustion, and helped her get Sebastian to the bathroom. Cleaning him broke her heart even more, because the bruises and cuts from the fight hadn't quite healed all the way, and she could see them fading. She hated he went through all this pain on her behalf. She *hated* what she had dragged him into, but... maybe they could make it through. Charlotte was right, they had to think positively, because doing anything else wasn't going to change the outcome of this scenario. If Sebastian hated her, then he hated her. There wasn't much she'd be able to do to change his mind, not at first anyway. But maybe he wouldn't. Maybe he would understand what happened and would have done the same had he been in their position.

After he was cleaned up, Charlotte dressed him in some of Victor's old clothes he kept there for traveling purposes. Laying him down on one of the beds, they merely sat and waited. Leona wished there was blood to drink anywhere in the apartment, but... there wasn't time for that. She didn't even know Charlotte had property here, and there certainly hadn't been a chance for her to stock up on blood bags in the fridge in case of an emergency. They would have to remedy that as soon as possible.

But as hungry as she was, she couldn't imagine not being there when Sebastian woke up. Not a chance. She wanted to be the *first* thing he saw. She wanted to welcome him into his new life with open arms.

Later, whether it was an hour or ten, Leona couldn't be sure, a thud sounded from the front door and they both shot up on the defensive. As they rushed into the other room to investigate, they were met with a bloodied and battered Victor, Whitney, and Piper.

Charlotte let out a cry of relief and was immediately in Victor's arms, kissing him as if she'd never done so before in her life. Leona had similar reactions to her two friends, so relieved that they were okay.

"How did you escape?" the redhead breathed, looking between them.

"Damien came," Whitney said. "Held him back while we left. I don't even want to think about…"

"Gideon won't hurt him," Piper said, in a tone like she'd reassured her a hundred times before this. "The priority and the *plan* was to get back here in one piece." She glanced toward the room Leona and Charlotte met them from. "Is he awake yet?"

"Not yet," Leona said with a sad look, shaking her head.

"He'll wake up," the blonde said firmly. "In the meantime, you look like a skeleton, which is saying something," she said, handing her the insulated bag slung over her shoulder. "We swung by the house before we came here. We knew he'd be starving you, and we figured you wouldn't be able to hunt from here.

Leona took the bag and looked inside, nearly crying in happiness. She snatched a blood bag out and immediately pierced it with her teeth, draining it in an instant. She went through five more before she felt sated enough to not lose her sanity. The others made quick work of the rest of the bags.

"What about when Bas wakes up?" Charlotte asked, throwing the last of the bags into the trash. "Should we go out and get more?"

"Bagged blood won't do shit for him," Piper said, cleaning her mouth up with a wet paper towel. "We will need to take him out to hunt. He probably won't be too pleased about that."

A few scoffs were heard around the room. Understatement of the century.

Leona sat in the armchair across from the bed Sebastian was laying in, where she'd been ever since she'd fed. Victor and Charlotte were in the room with her while Piper and Whitney kept watch outside near the door and windows. Leona was wringing her hands in wait, feeling like she was being eaten alive with the agony of all the anxiety coursing through her.

She closed her eyes and just focused, willing something, *anything* to happen.

After a few minutes of sitting there in silence, she flipped her eyes open and stared at her beloved. Charlotte and Victor both quirked their heads to her, then to him. They had heard the same thing she did.

Him.

Leona sat up and leaned forward, bracing her hands on the edge of the mattress. If she could breathe, the air would be hitched in her throat. Her green eyes flicked back and forth over the features on his face, searching for any sign of movement.

Whitney and Piper came into the room next, hovering in the doorway. All eyes were on the dark-haired man who hadn't moved in nearly a day.

Then, Sebastian's eyes fluttered open, his once dark eyes having turned a bright crimson red. He didn't move his body, just his eyes, as he adjusted. He could see the flecks of dust on the ceiling, floating in the air. He could hear cars whirring outside, specific conversations of those in buildings nearby, the breathing of the people within the block, the creaking of the bed beneath him…

"Sebastian."

He turned his head and met those familiar eyes of the woman he loved. Everything was different though. He *saw* her now. He saw every pore on her perfect porcelain skin. He saw the details in her irises, how long her eyelashes were, the fabric on the material of her clothing, each individual hair atop her head, her eyebrows, everywhere. Her voice even sounded different. It was as if each sound wave from every syllable was reverberating within his head.

Pushing himself up, he nearly catapulted off the bed with the force and speed. He parted his lips, his throat never having felt drier in his life. Bringing his hand up, he touched his neck, noting how cold it felt now. His hand then trailed down to his chest, where he remembered Gideon shoving his hand into. There was nothing but hardness there now. Not muscle, *hardness*. Like he was made of stone.

"I'm…" Sebastian started, not quite able to find his voice yet.

"Yes," Leona said, the others silent as they watched on. "You are. It was the only way."

"Gideon?" he questioned, looking at all of them, then settling his gaze on Leona. At her pained look, he knew they had not won. How had they gotten out? What happened? What *happened*? "Where are we?"

"New York," Charlotte answered. "My house."

He looked around and recognized everything then. His head was swimming. He felt the sheets beneath him, noting all the new sensations gracing his fingertips, his hands. He swallowed thickly, then looked to Leona. "You did this."

"I did," Charlotte chimed, before Leona could respond. "I did this. You were going to die."

Sebastian pressed his lips together in a thin line and wasn't sure how to respond. He looked back at Leona and shook his head. "Why are we not at home?"

"We can't go back there," Leona said sadly. "Not for a long time."

"Sebastian," Piper said, stepping forward. "We need to catch you up to speed on everything."

"Where is Gideon?" Sebastian asked, ignoring Piper.

"We don't know. We escaped but he'll be looking for us. You need to listen to us though. You need to feed. You won't be in your right mind until—"

"Why didn't you let me die?"

Leona frowned painfully. "We… Seb, I—"

"*Don't* call me that," Sebastian hissed, pushing himself off the bed. He swayed a bit, then braced himself against the wall. He did feel weak. But stronger than he ever had. It was strange. "Take me back to the castle. I'm going to kill that fucker. Once and for all."

"Sit down," Piper snapped, her temper gone. She shoved him back on the bed, the wood splintering in protest. "You aren't doing shit until you get fed. You didn't die. You're one of us and the quicker you get used to that and stop blaming everyone else, the quicker we can figure out how the hell to hide from Gideon."

"I'm not hiding—"

"Sebastian," Victor interrupted. "Listen to her."

"No," Leona said, looking between them all. "There are things you don't know about. Things Gideon told me… about you," she said, her eyes settling on Sebastian. "You're much more rooted in our world than you think, Sebastian."

"What?" he asked, shaking his head. "What do you mean?"

"Gideon said he recognized you somehow when he first saw you. Admittedly, I did too. I thought it was just our love laying dormant, but… he did some digging, and your great-great… however many greats *something* was a vampire hunter. One that nearly took Gideon out."

"You're waiting until *now* to tell me this?!" Sebastian gawked.

"I didn't know... Or at least, I didn't remember. He showed me in the cell. It's part of the reason he's so obsessed with making a show of killing you, beyond punishing me. And I think he's worried if you became immortal, you'd..."

"Be able to kill him," Sebastian finished. "Well, wish fucking granted."

"Sebastian, he's much stronger than you, you don't know what you're doing," Leona protested. "You heard him. He wants you for himself. Any other scenario, you wouldn't survive. I'm begging you, stay away from him... We can run away. There are ways to keep him in the dark." She stepped toward him, but stopped as Sebastian flinched. It caused a pain so deep within her, it was almost foreign. "Please..."

"Stop," Charlotte said, shaking her head. "We don't need to talk about any of this right now. We need to get blood into Sebastian so he doesn't get pissed off and accidentally kill us all. Then we can talk about a plan of action."

Sebastian looked around at them, then shook his head. "I'm not *doing* that."

"You don't have a choice," Piper said, yanking him off the bed again. He struggled, but she was stronger. "Come on. We're going to show you how to hunt, then you can be pissed off at us for however long you want. You have an eternity to do so."

Sebastian wrenched his arm from her grip and kept his

distance from them. As he thought about everything, knowing this was the hand he'd been dealt, he… wasn't sure what to do. He never wanted to be a monster. He loved Leona, he *thought* he had, but… this was different. Had it all been for nothing? Gideon was still alive. They had Leona, yes, but there was still a threat looming over them, suffocating them at every turn.

But then again… if he trained, fed, got strong… and if what Leona said was true… then maybe he *could* be the one to break the curse.

As the rest of the immortals around him gathered by the door, he huffed out a breath.

Fuck it.

End of Book One.

Read on for an exclusive sneak peek at the first chapter of the second and final installment of the *Blood* series, *Bloodstained*.

"If you want to talk about anything — if you have any questions — please feel free to…"

"I'm fine."

Sebastian walked next to Leona, hoping she didn't continue to press him about what had happened. He was still processing things himself. His senses were overwhelmed with all the new data they were taking in. Perhaps New York City wasn't the greatest place for a new vampire — a reluctant one at that — to learn the ropes of immortality.

"Homeless might be the best option. There's a camp not far from here, near Queens," Charlotte explained as they navigated side streets and alleys together.

"A mass murder might not be the best plan," Piper chimed in. "Let's just focus on getting Sebastian fed. We can all get our own later. He's the priority right now. And we need to stay together anyway. We don't know who could be lurking and if… *he* is currently on the hunt for us."

Sebastian scoffed under his breath.

"Something you'd like to add?" Piper snapped.

"I think it's pretty fucking likely he's hunting for us. Namely me," Sebastian said. "I'm surprised you didn't have a wooden stake waiting for me when I woke up. How long did it take you to come up with that bullshit story about me being some *chosen* vampire hunter?"

"Sebastian," Leona sighed, a pained frown on her face. "It's not bullshit. You were going to die if I didn't... if *we* didn't..."

"I don't care," Sebastian interrupted. It felt as if his throat were closing in on itself. This hunger — or thirst, more accurately — wasn't like what he felt as a human. His stomach didn't turn into knots or rumble, he just felt... irritated, dry, *parched*. He wondered if he'd forget what things felt like as a human as time went on. Had Leona? He would never be able to experience sunlight again, or alcohol, or sleep, or any of the things he enjoyed on a regular basis.

"Stop," Charlotte said as she put her hand out, making everyone halt in their tracks. She pointed forward, a small light illuminated in the distance. Sebastian could see movement. His eyesight had never been so crisp. They were at least a hundred yards away. "That's the homeless camp," the blonde said, looking at them. "I'm sure we can find some that have broken off from the group for Sebastian."

"Let him hunt," Victor said nonchalantly. Heads turned to him and he folded his arms, shrugging his broad shoulders. "He's already pissed off. Let him do what he wants. We can clean the mess up later."

"Need I remind you we're depending on an element of *discreetness*?!" Whitney hissed, her eyes flashing angrily. "Letting Sebastian run wild is going to draw unnecessary attention to us. If Gid—" she paused, swallowing at the looks she received. His name had garnered too much power in their group. "If *he* catches wind there's vampires here, and he shows up, it won't take him long to sniff us out. We need a plan. No more reckless behavior."

Victor lolled his head to one side, keeping his arms crossed. "Fine. You know best."

"Thank you," Whitney said, before turning to the space where Sebastian was. Her face blanched and her eyes erratically began scanning the area. "Where did Sebastian go?!"

Sebastian was lurking on the outskirts of the camp, watching multiple people gather around a fire, laugh, talk, enjoy life together. He frowned to himself, then rested his head against the wall he was standing by. These people were normal. They were innocent. They hadn't hurt anyone. They didn't *deserve* what his 'friends' wanted to do to them.

He felt like a hypocrite. He had been fine to turn the other cheek to Leona and the rest hunting, feeding, *killing*, but now that he was faced with it, he felt disgusted with himself.

Though, he understood now the pull of his thirst. Even in his horror, he was having to physically restrain himself from walking toward them and ripping each of their throats open. Was that what life would be now? Misery until he couldn't take it any longer? Leona had mentioned feeding off animals, but that their blood wouldn't fully satisfy any healthy immortal, and that craving would always be present.

If only his father were still alive. He'd gladly travel to

the bottom of the country and drain every drop from his worthless body.

"We don't have to do this here."

Sebastian quirked his head, seeing Leona's flaming locks out of the corner of his eye.

Turning his attention back to the people, he didn't respond.

Leona approached him, then carefully placed a hand on his shoulder. She tried to ignore the slight flinch from him, and chalked it up to him just being in shock. She couldn't afford to think any other way.

There was *no way* she could lose him, not after all this. He was angry, rightfully so, and she wanted to make things better. She wanted to nurture him and give him whatever he needed, no matter how long the transition process took. He wasn't even turning to her, which broke her heart into a thousand pieces. She had barely gotten to touch him since he woke up. He hadn't wanted her near him. The entire walk here was awkward, and if it wasn't silent, it was filled with a snarky and resentful quip from him about how he hadn't asked for any of this. About how she'd betrayed him.

"We can go somewhere else. But you *do* need to feed. Your head will clear and we'll be able to talk about everything. I know this is a huge change — one you never asked for — but this is the hand we've been dealt. *You've* been dealt. Let me help you. I know exactly how you're feeling. And I wish I had had someone who had my best interests at heart holding my hand to guide me," she said, trailing her hand from his shoulder, down his arm, to his fingers.

Sebastian stayed there for a moment, then pulled his hand away from her. "You've done enough."

With that, he went back to the group, who had caught up nearby. Leona closed her eyes and resisted crying out. There weren't many times in her life she'd felt so damn helpless.

She more than understood why he was angry, and she knew she didn't have a choice but to let him work through it, but a part of her worried that he never *would* work through it. She worried he would despise her for the rest of their existence.

She felt incredibly selfish for worrying about that at a time like this.

"Charlie," Sebastian said, eyeing his best friend. "I want to go with you."

"We'll all—" Victor started, but stopped at Sebastian's expression.

"No. Just Charlie. I just want to be with her," Sebastian pressed.

Charlotte looked between them, her gaze landing on Leona. At the redhead's slight nod of permission, the vampire's light eyes went back to Sebastian. "Okay, Sebby. Let's go."

About the author

Kerrigan Bailey Casimir is a former journalist-turned-author with a passion for romance and all things weird. She grew up in Panama City Beach, Florida, but moved to New Orleans, Louisiana in her twenties with her wife Amber. Though she has a background on the sandy beaches of the Florida Panhandle, she grew up attending Saints games and exploring the French Quarter in New Orleans with her family.

An Ole Miss graduate (Hotty Toddy!), Kerrigan has dedicated most of her life to honing her craft and delving into the nuances of storytelling. She started her literary journey by writing fanfiction with her best friend, Becca Prince; that love for stories led her to a career in journalism, where she was trained in formal writing, photography, videography, and auditory storytelling.

Outside of the writing realm, Kerrigan can be found running around New Orleans with a camera in her hand, capturing all the best moments for tourists and locals alike. When she's off the clock, she enjoys a yummy cocktail and dinner with her wife, and coming home to all her animals.

Kerrigan's debut novel, *Bloodlust*, is a love letter to her best friend, Becca, who tragically died on May 15th, 2023. Kerrigan has taken some of their stories they created together and carefully woven them into Sebastian and Leona's tale of love and misery. Her relationship and writing style are prevalent within her works of art and can always be traced back to the unbreakable bond she had with her platonic soulmate.

Connect with Kerrigan on the Internet and social media through her website, kbcasimir.com, or on Instagram and TikTok at @kbcasimir to stay updated on future projects and her current work.

Acknowledgements

Hello to my friends, family, and readers — I could not do this without you.

First and foremost, I want to thank my biggest cheerleader who has never stopped believing in me, and pushed me to be the best version of myself: my wife Amber. Sweetheart, you are my forever muse and I am the luckiest person in existence to get to call you mine. I worship every second I get to spend with you.

Secondly, I want to thank my family: my sister Kennedy, my mom Wendi, and my dad Mike. Your support for me as a writer over the years — even when I used to hide it and pretend I was just aimlessly scrolling through Tumblr (which, I sort of was) — has always driven me to continue doing what I love. Writing puts me in an extremely vulnerable state, and you have taken me seriously from day one. I love y'all with everything in me.

Thirdly, I want to thank my best friends: Ashley, Shelby, Nathan, and Amanda. Y'all have watched me grow as a person, journalist, writer, creator, photographer, and probably a million other things. You have been there with me at my lowest lows and highest highs. I have used all of you as a crutch when I couldn't stand on my own, and for that, I'll never be able to repay you. Thank you for building me up when I didn't think I was good enough. You are my rocks.

Fourthly, I want to take another moment to thank my dearest and most special person in the history of my life, Becca, for making me the writer I am today. This book, this *journey*, would not be possible without you, and I wish so desperately you were here to take the ride with me. I miss you to my core every second of every day. You are one of the loves of my life and I will never have another person connect with me like you do. You have shaped me as a child, a teenager, an adult, and a professional. I wish we could have grown old together like we planned, with both of our kids running around and loving all the things we love together and becoming the best of friends just like we were. But I'm endlessly grateful for the chance to grow *up* together. Forever 29, I adore you in eternity *always*.

And lastly, I want to thank you, the reader, for supporting me in this endeavor. Thank you for taking a chance on this novel, and I hope you enjoyed your trip to Louisiana enough to follow my trek through authorhood as long as it lasts. The impact you have on me knows no bounds, and you keep me grinding, going, and striving to be better.

Cheers,
Kerrigan xoxo

Made in the USA
Columbia, SC
27 July 2024

39259324R00164